EXIL   ⌐⌐∨ S

BOOKS 1-4

HOPE FORD

FREE BOOKS

Want FREE BOOKS?
Go to www.authorhopeford.com/freebies

SNIPER

1

AVERY

I STAND AT THE GATE, LOOKING AT THE BIG tattooed man with the oily hair and wonder if I made the mistake of running from one evil to another.

He sneers at me and the way he glances down my body has my stomach rolling.

"Jeremy Johnson. He has to be here. Can you please check?" I plead with him again. If he's not here, I don't know what I'll do... where I'll go. I don't have any money left. Not after I bought the bus ticket and ate some food on the way here. Two dollars and sixty-five cents. That's all the money I have to my name. Regardless of how little I have, I know I can't go back where I came from. I'll be dead the minute I walk in the door.

The dirty man grabs his crotch and thrusts his

hips at me. "Honey, there's no Jeremy Johnson here. But I'll help you… I'm just the man you need."

He takes a step toward me and when I go to pull away, he grabs on to my wrist. I almost faint then. I can feel the dizziness about to take over and I can't stop the thoughts in my head asking, *Is this really it? Did I survive all of that only to end up here in this position?* I've had about all I can take. I've survived the last few weeks and when I finally got away, I came straight here. It was the only place I could think of, straight to the only man that I thought I could trust to help me.

My older brother, Allen, served in the army with Jeremy Johnson. They kept in touch through the years and when my brother got sick, right before he passed away, he told me that if I ever needed someone, Jeremy would help me. Well, at the time, I didn't think anything of it. But now, he's the one and only person that I've thought about since I ran from my husband.

I was eighteen when I got married. I thought I loved him and the first year of our marriage was fine. However, by the second, he started getting mad all the time and taking it out on me. I've lost count of how many times I've been in the hospital. You would think that someone would be suspicious, someone would help me. But that wasn't the case. My husband, I found out only recently, is a drug trafficker. And he controls half the town.

I couldn't leave him, I couldn't divorce him and no one would help me. After my last beating, he left me with no one watching me. I started paying attention to his routine. And like always, after he beats me, he leaves the house. He's usually only gone a few hours. I guess he figures if he beats me enough, I will be unconscious for a while. Well, this time I was ready. I egged him on.

I told him I was going to get a job. He flew off the handle, like I knew he would. He started screaming and instead of hunkering down, I started talking back. I wanted him to beat me. That was the only way I would be able to escape... as crazy as that sounds. As soon as he left the house, I left my phone and all my clothes, stole one of his cars out of the garage and drove two towns over to hop on a bus. I had made sure the timing would be perfect so I wouldn't have to hang around. The only thing I brought with me was some money I had been skimming off the grocery bill and the address for Jeremy Johnson. That's it. I didn't pack a bag. He would have noticed and I didn't take time to grab anything else.

I look up into the soulless man's eyes as his hand grips the back of my neck. My whole body tenses, knowing I don't want this to happen, but knowing I don't have the strength to stop it.

"Prospect, what are you doing?"

At the sound of another man's voice, I have a renewed energy and start to struggle.

"Let her go… Now!" the man towering over the both of us demands.

I'm instantly released and I barely stay upright on my feet.

The man that was holding me only moments ago starts muttering, "She's here looking for a Jeremy Johnson. There's no man here by that name. I figure she was sent by the Kings and I was going to rough her up and send her back where she belongs, Brick."

I can barely focus on what the man is saying, I'm too caught up in the beast of a man staring down at me. He's huge and I realize now that I have no chance of getting out of here alive. My shoulders drop and my legs start to give out.

"Prospect, I don't care who you think sent her, we never touch a woman that doesn't want to be touched. If you're wanting to join the Exiled Guardians, that's one of the first things you should know about us." He starts walking toward me and I sway on my feet.

He leans down and puts an arm under my legs, picking me up like I don't weigh anything. "It's okay, honey. No one will hurt you here," he whispers down to me. He looks up at the man he called Prospect. "And Jeremy Johnson is Sniper. I don't know who she is but you better pray the pres doesn't kill you for what you just did to her."

He walks away then with me in his arms. He was gruff talking to Prospect but with me, his voice softens. "It's okay, honey. I'm going to take you to Sniper, or uh, Jeremy. I'm Brick and I promise…"

But I don't hear him. I pass out as he walks through the entrance with me in his arms.

2

SNIPER

THE KNOCK ON MY OFFICE DOOR BARELY RESONATES before it swings open and in walks Brick, our sergeant in arms, with a curvy bundle in his arms.

With only one glance at her, I can feel the blood in my veins throbbing. My hands fist at my sides. Am I jealous of my brother? Fuck yeah, I am.

"Do you have to knock them out to get them to come home with you now, Brick?" I ask him.

He walks over to the couch. "Har, har, Pres. Nope, this little bundle is for you. Came to the gate asking for you. Prospect roughed her up a little, but I don't think he caused the bruises. I think they were there before she got here."

I jump out of my seat. "Did he knock her out?"

He shakes his head. "No, she passed out while I was carrying her in here. She was barely able to stand upright on her feet."

He lays her down gently so as to not jostle her. She doesn't wake. She instantly curls to her side with her hands between her knees and buries herself deeper into the couch.

Brick and I stand over her and I have to stop myself from reaching over and waking her up to demand who gave her the bruises. Her lip is swollen and her eye is black and blue, but none of that takes away from her beauty. Her long red hair is in tangles over her shoulder and even though she's curled up, I can tell she is short, probably a foot shorter than my six foot three inch frame. She has a curvy body and I want to trace my hand over the curve of her hip so bad I can almost feel it.

She moves a little as if she's trying to get comfortable and she grimaces, making me wonder where else she may be hurt.

"Do you know her?"

I turn to the man beside me. I had forgotten he was still here. Brick is looking down at her and there is pity in his expression. He's a big brute of a man so the compassion on his face would surprise some people. Not me though. We served together in the army years ago. I've seen him kill a man with his bare hands then pick up a child and carry him ten miles through a war zone to get him to safety.

I shake my head side to side. "No. I don't know her. You said she was asking for me?"

He nods. "Yep, well, actually for Jeremy Johnson. The prospect didn't know that name so he was messing with her."

"What do you mean, 'messing with her'?"

"He thought the Kings had sent one of their women over to mess with us. I don't know really. When I showed up she was struggling to get out of his grasp."

I walk over to my desk and gesture for him to follow me. "Which prospect was it?"

His lips flatten. "Blade."

I probably could have guessed. We've had problems with Blade since he started. "Get rid of him. We don't treat women like that. Hell, we don't even treat the sweet butts that way. Make an example of him before he goes."

Everyone, member and prospect alike of the Exiled Guardians, knows that we don't touch women. We are a group of law abiding men, well, for the most part anyway. We run legit businesses. The bar, the strip club, the bike shop and the tattoo parlor. But we are still a biker club and family and brotherhood runs in our veins.

Brick nods his head, but I can see the question in his eyes before he even asks. "What about her? What are we going to do with her? Do you think she is bringing trouble with her?"

I merely nod. Yep, no man is going to give her up without a fight and I'm assuming that's who gave her the bruises.

Brick shrugs his shoulders confidently. "We'll be ready."

When Brick walks out of the room, I go back to the couch and sit down on the coffee table looking at her. She's young. Really young. Right now, I'm praying that she's at least legal because the thoughts going through my head could get me put into prison if not.

Hours go by and she's still asleep. I tried to get some work done but I kept finding myself over next to her. Now, I'm sitting at the end of the couch with her feet in my lap. I discarded her shoes a while ago and the sight of her pretty pink toes has my lower belly pulling in need.

She stretches, her arms over her head, pulling her shirt up and baring her midriff to me. Her feet press into my lap and when they glide by my cock, I'm instantly hard from the contact.

I can't take my eyes off of her. All of a sudden she jerks and raises her head to look around. Looking back at me are the greenest eyes I've ever seen. I had wondered while she was sleeping what color they would be.

She sits up on the couch and slides her feet underneath her, burying herself against the other end.

I hold my hands up in front of myself, palms facing her. "It's okay. I'm Sniper… I'm Jeremy. I won't hurt you."

"You're Jeremy Johnson?" she stutters.

I nod my head at her, still trying not to make any sudden movements.

"Yes, they said you were here to see me," I tell her in a quiet voice.

She jumps off the couch. "Yeah, yeah, that's right, but I've made a mistake. I'm just going to go now."

I stand up to my full height and she lays her head back to look up at me. "It's okay, precious. No one is going to hurt you here."

She laughs, more of a scared giggle. "Yeah, right, I've already been manhandled by your gate keeper. I think it's probably best if I leave now."

"Blade is not a member of the club. He was a prospect and he has already been removed. He won't bother you again. You won't even have to see him."

She turns her head to the side. "You fired him? Or killed him? What does that mean exactly… Forget it, I don't want to know."

She starts walking toward the door and I don't want to grab her and scare her. I move in front of her. "Honey, normally I would tell you that's club business, but I'll make an exception for you today. We didn't kill him. We kicked him out. If he treated you like that, we don't want him here. That's not what we're about." She moves to the side and I step in front of her again. "Now, listen, I'm not letting you leave until I know you're going to be okay. You came asking around for me. How do you know me?"

"I don't," she confesses. She brushes her hair off her shoulders and I see the handprints around her neck for the first time. "My brother knows you —well, he did."

I take a step closer to her. "Okay. Three questions. One, who's your brother?" I run my hand down the side of her face. "Two, who did this to you? And three, what's your name?"

3

AVERY

I SHOULD RUN. I KNOW I SHOULD. HE'S A BIG MAN, not as big as the one that carried me in here, but big enough that I know if he wanted to hurt me, he could. Of course, with the gentle touch of his hand on my cheek, it doesn't feel like he wants to hurt me. But even I know that doesn't mean he won't.

He's looking straight at me and I can see the anger on his face. I take a step back out of reach.

"I'm not going to talk to you when you're already pissed off at me. Can I just go? Please?" I ask him as I try to walk around him again.

He stops me again, takes a deep breath and rolls his shoulders backwards like he's trying to relax. "I'm not pissed at you. I'm pissed at whoever put those marks on your face and neck."

"What if I deserved it?" I almost scream at him.

there were five other women looking at me as if I've kicked them out of their bed for the night… by the way, are these sheets clean?"

He outright laughs at my question. "They're clean."

I open my mouth to ask him again about the women, but then slam it shut. It's none of my business. I just have to keep reminding myself of that.

"And I haven't had a Twinkie in here – or anywhere else – in a long while."

I don't respond to him and instead of looking at him across the pillow, I close my eyes. The silence is comfortable. That is until he asks me the question I've been dreading.

"Tell me about your husband."

I don't open my eyes. With them closed, I feel a sense of security and I need that more than anything when I talk about him.

"We got married when I was eighteen. The first year was okay, but somewhere along the line, he got mixed up with drugs and the wrong people. He started beating me. He beat me more times than I could count. We live in a small town and people at the hospital even looked the other way when it was obvious he was beating me. Nobody goes against Cameron. Well, anyway, he had created a pattern. He would beat me, usually until I passed out, and then he would leave the house and be gone for hours. I guess he thought I wasn't able to go anywhere so he never worried about me leaving. Those were the only times I was ever alone. Anytime else, he was with me, or had someone with me. So, this last time, I forced myself to get up. I stole one of his cars, drove two towns over and got on a bus for here."

He asks me a few more questions about his name, his work and the name of the town. I answer him truthfully, but I also worry about him getting involved.

"Look, Jeremy, I don't want you to do anything. That's not what this is about. I just need somewhere to stay until I can get on my feet again. That's all. He doesn't know anything about you and he won't come here."

Sniper

I CAN HEAR it in her voice that she honestly believes that. Maybe that's good though. I want her to feel safe, and as long as she's here, she will be.

She doesn't realize that a man like him, one that beats women, is not going to be okay with her running from him. It would be easy to trace where she went on a bus. And this town is small too, not that a lot of people would go against the Exiled

Guardians. But there's still a possibility he will be able to find her.

When the silence is weighing on me, I realize I don't want her to go to sleep talking about her husband. "So, in here, or just the two of us, I'm Jeremy. Out there, I'm Sniper."

"Oh." She pulls the covers up farther across her shoulders. "I'm sorry. I wasn't thinking. I can call you Sniper all the time."

"No. No, I like when you call me Jeremy," I admit to her. I can't remember the last time I heard my birth name before she called me that earlier today. But from her, it just sounds right.

"Can I ask you something?"

"Sure."

"I don't know a lot about motorcycle gangs," she starts.

"Clubs. We're not a gang. It's a club."

"Oh, okay, so I don't know a lot about motor-cycle clubs. Earlier when you told your club that I was yours and under club protection, well, that seemed pretty heavy. Not only to me, but by the looks on some of their faces, them too. What does that mean?"

Fuck, I should have known she wouldn't miss that. And although I'm still working out how I feel, I'm not good at putting feelings into words. I've never had to before. My longest relationship has been when I let a woman sleep in my bed overnight. And even that hardly ever happened.

All I know is that I've never felt this territorial before. I've never claimed a woman before and she's right: surprise was on their faces. I just knew that I wasn't going to stand by and wait for someone else to claim her. Ever since I saw her curvy body in Brick's arms, I wanted her. But it's a different kind of want. It makes my heart pound in my ears and blood throb in my veins.

But do I tell her all that? She's here, under my protection, and I don't want to scare her off. I shrug my shoulders in the dark room. "You've been through enough. You don't need the men, even though they're good men, fighting over you. I declared you as mine. You're off limits now. You can heal… take time and get better."

"Oh," she mumbles.

I try to look at her face, but the shadows have it hidden from me. Was that disappointment I heard in her voice?

"Get some sleep. I'll be here in the morning. We have church, so if you can't find me that's where I'll be."

She stretches her arms over her head and yawns. When she settled again, she asks, "Is tomorrow Sunday? I thought it was Friday. How long was I out for?"

I chuckle. I swear I've laughed more with her in

one day than I have in months. "Church is just a club meeting. It's in the big room next to my office. It's patched members only, but if you need me someone can get me for you."

"Okay." She yawns again. "Good night."

"Night."

5

AVERY

I SLEPT BETTER LAST NIGHT THAN I HAVE IN A lifetime. At one point in the middle of the night, I rolled over and wrapped myself around Jeremy. He seems to have slept through it, but the heat and safety of his arms almost has me wishing I would have stayed there. Once I moved away, I felt a cold chill the rest of the night.

I stretch and rise up on the bed, looking around the bare room. Besides the large bed and dresser, there's not much else to it. There are some shopping bags on the dresser with a note attached. I get out of bed and the chill hits me so I wrap the blanket around me and pad over to the dresser.

Picking up the note, I read, "I had one of the twinkies get you some clothes. I'll take you shopping later for more and whatever else you need. Don't leave the clubhouse."

I roll my eyes thinking really, where the hell am I going to go?

I pull the tags off my new clothes and thank goodness there's even a new package of underwear. There's a bra, but I guess they were being cute and bought me a 36A, knowing good and well that that's not what I wear. I put on my bra from yesterday, and then pull the shirt out of the bag. It's a T-shirt with a cat on the front of it. Really? Who picked this shit out? Oh well, at least it fits. Next I pull out the new pair of jeans and when I see the size fourteen on the tag, I wad them up and throw them back in the bag. I walk over to my clothes I had on yesterday and slip on my size eighteen jeans. At least they put in a toothbrush. After taking care of business in the bathroom, I slide on my sandals and open the door to hopefully get something to eat and maybe see Jeremy.

As soon as I open the door, I see a man standing there with his arms across his chest. "Hey, I'm Rancher."

"Uh, I'm Avery." I look up at him with his cowboy hat and the tattoos up and down his arms. Okay, he's a cowboy in a motorcycle club. Maybe that's normal, what do I know? "Did you need something?"

"Nope."

I nod at him and start walking toward the

kitchen but stop when I see he's following me. "Uh, what are you doing?"

The corners of his lips curve up just slightly, but just as quickly they flatten out. "Sniper told me to keep an eye on you. Make sure no one bothered you."

I nod my head at him. "Aren't you supposed to be at church?"

He lifts his shoulder in a shrug. "He made an exception."

My stomach growls then and Rancher's face breaks out into a big smile. "We better get you fed."

My face heats, but I simply follow him to the kitchen.

Sniper

"OKAY, so does everyone have it? Brick, you're going lead on this. Me, Rancher, and Rider will go with you. I want him finished along with anyone that gets in our way."

Brick stands up. "Got it, Pres. Widowmaker in effect. After seeing Avery yesterday, this is an easy order to enforce. We ride out in one hour."

"Church dismissed," I call out and watch as everyone stands to leave. "Hey, Brick, if Avery's up, have Rancher bring her here for me."

"Got it," he calls out.

I watch as everyone files out of the room. I didn't talk to Avery about any of this, and I don't know if I will. I did what I thought needed done. I'm not used to answering to anyone. Having her in my bed all night, I barely slept. At one point she curled up against me and I had to fight hard to not wrap my arms around her and pull her into me. It would have been so easy to pull her up on top of me. But I stopped myself. When it happens, and hell yeah, it's going to happen, I don't want anything, namely her husband, hanging over her head.

Rancher walks in a while later and Avery is following behind. She has two plates in her hands. She smiles up at Rancher and thanks him before he shuts the door.

She walks over to the table and sets a plate of bacon, eggs and toast down in front of me. She takes the seat across from me. "I asked Keeper and he didn't know if you ate or not, so I fixed you a plate."

I smile at her. "Thanks, honey. Nice shirt."

She rolls her eyes. "Beggars can't be choosers, right?"

"I was going to take you shopping but I have to take a trip. I'll only be gone a day — two max — but if you order some stuff online just overnight it."

"I'll just wash my clothes. I'm fine. Where are you going?"

I shake my head at her. "That's not how this works, honey. I tell you to do something and you do it."

She laughs. Literally laughs at me. Fuck, I'm going to have to get used to this. So she doesn't like to be told what to do. Okay.

I open my laptop and carry it around the table. I sit down next to her, opening a website to a shopping site. "I have to get on the road soon. Pick out some damn clothes."

She eats a piece of bacon, then wipes her hands off before going through and picking a few things. Once she's done, I add a few different styles of what she picked out and add quantity to the jeans. "What about shoes? You can't live in flip flops."

She punches a few buttons and adds a pair to the cart. I go in after her and add a few more.

"Okay, what about underwear, bathroom stuff, anything like that?"

She adds a few things and then I look at the cart, adding some more before hitting buy it now.

"Sniper, no, I'll never be able to repay you," she complains at the price.

I grip her chin softly and turn her face toward me and away from the computer. "What happened to calling me Jeremy?" I like her calling me by my given name.

"Sorry, everyone was calling you Sniper all morning. It just came out."

I nod. "Okay, well, you don't owe me a thing. I told you I was going to take care of things and I am. But while I'm gone I need you to stay at the clubhouse. I have everything laid out in my office, and if you feel like it, I would appreciate you filing and cleaning up a little in there." I thought about it all night and I know she's the type that has to stay busy. That's the only way I'm going to keep her here at this point… at least until I get back. I locked up all the files that didn't need to be seen; everything else she can sort and go through.

She takes another bite of her food. "Sure, no problem. But you never answered me."

I finish eating mine and push the plate away from me. "It's club business," I tell her. Which is the truth: after church this morning, it became club business.

"So does club business mean you can't tell me about it?"

I shake my head. This one is going to test me for sure. "Club business means I can't talk about it. It means the less you know the better."

In a small voice, she asks me, "Does it mean it's dangerous? Are you coming back?"

I slide her chair around so she's facing me. She looks at me briefly then looks away. I can see the fear on her face and I wish I could wipe it away.

"It's not dangerous. Not this time. And yes, I'm coming back."

Her shoulders drop and she takes a deep breath. "Okay, can you tell me if this has anything to do with me?"

I cup her cheek with my hand. Her bruises are already fading, but I still can't get the image of her bloodied lip and bruised eyes out of my head. "I'm not playing the guessing game with you. All you need to know is that I'm taking care of things. I will be safe while doing it and I am always going to come back to you."

"Always?" she asks as her eyes fly up to mine.

I lean my forehead against hers. "Always. When I get back, we have some things to talk about. But I need to know you're safe. No running off. And I want you in my bed at night. Tatts is going to keep an eye on you until I'm back."

A knock sounds on the door, and I hear Brick holler, "Ready, Pres?"

I pull away from Avery and stand up. "Be right there," I tell him. "Be good while I'm gone," I say to Avery and stride over to the door.

"Wait," she says and runs across the room to me. Her arms go around my waist and she squeezes me tight. "Will you kiss me before you go, Jeremy?"

I grip on to her shoulders and look down into her darkened green eyes. I bend down and when my lips touch hers it's like a force binds us together.

My hands slide down her back and pull her tighter against me. Her mouth, soft and nimble under mine, opens wider and I increase the pressure of my tongue stroking her mouth. The more I give her, the more she takes, until we're both breathing heavily and I have to force myself to pull away from her.

"I'll be back, I promise." I kiss her briefly one more time and leave. I don't look back, don't let myself, because I know if I do, I won't be able to walk out the door.

6

AVERY

It's been two days since he left. He told me that it would be a max of two days and every time the door opens, I look up to see if it's him or not. I found out that he took Brick, Rancher and Rider with him. But other than that, no one is talking.

I've stayed close to the clubhouse. I go out to the yard a few times a day, but other than that I've been holed up here. I sleep in his bed every night. I probably would have done that anyway, even if he didn't tell me to. I found that it makes me feel closer to him.

Right now, there's another party going on. I've decided to put myself to work. It took a lot of convincing for Tatts to let me work the bar, but Keeper finally assured him that he would keep his eye on me. But honestly, I haven't had any trouble. Everyone has been super nice to me since Sniper made his announcement. Even the sweet butts stay away from me.

I slide a jack and Coke over to Tatts and his old lady, Nova. He has his arms around her and she's smiling up at him. Honestly, they seem to be night and day. Where he's tattooed and angry looking a lot of the time, she is more like "the girl next door" and always smiling. Watching them and the way they look at each other makes me miss Sniper even more. I start wiping down the counter when I feel someone staring at me. When I look up, Sniper is standing behind me at the doorway of the kitchen. He must have come in the back way.

Although I should play it cool, I can't. The smile that comes on my face stretches wide, causing my cheeks to pull and tighten.

But that's okay, because he's smiling back at me in the same way.

I walk over to him and glance up and down his body as I go. Either to just look at him, or to make sure he's all right, I'm not sure which.

"You're back."

His hand goes around to the back of my neck. "I promised you I would be. I see you found a way to keep busy."

I shrug my shoulders. "I had to, I was going crazy. Plus, Tatts said it would be okay with you as long as I stayed behind the bar."

His hand tightens on me. "That was smart of Tatt. C'mon, honey. I need you in my arms."

He tugs me but I stop him. "I told Keeper I would help him tonight. I don't think I can just leave."

He shakes his head at me and then hollers over my head, "Hey, Keep! We're out."

"Okay, Pres. Thanks for your help, Avery."

I wave at Keeper and snicker at the control Sniper has here. The man definitely gets what he wants.

I follow him down the hallway to his room. He goes straight to the bed and sits down, pulling me between his legs.

"What about Brick, Rancher and Rider? They okay?" I ask him, just remembering that I didn't see them come back.

He nods his head. "They're fine. They wanted to stop at a bar an hour out of town. I wanted to get back to you."

I smile at him. "I'm glad you did. I was worried about you."

"I figured you would be, and well, that's not something I'm used to." His hands grip my hips until I'm standing snug between his legs. "What's wrong, honey? Did something happen while I was gone?"

I shake my head side to side. I put my hands on his shoulders and the feel of his thick muscles under my fingers has me squeezing on to him. I take a deep breath, trying to build up my courage. "I told myself that if you came back, that I was not going to let Cameron stand in the way of what I want anymore. I told myself that even though you could have any sweet butt out there and I don't look anything like them, I would still not let that hold me back. I just…"

"What is it? Tell me, honey."

I look into his eyes and I know I can trust him. "I want you, Jeremy."

His eyes glare into me, almost like he's looking for something on my face, like he's trying to read me.

"Are you sure? We don't have to. I rushed home and figured I would be happy to just hold you again. I wasn't expecting this."

"I mean, we don't have to. I just wanted you to know, that's all," I mutter to him. Rejection pierces my heart.

He must notice my face drop, because he tugs me up onto his lap until I'm straddling him with my knees on the bed.

"I want you. Those women out there have nothing on you. You're the one I want. But I wanted to give you time. To make sure this is what you want."

"You're what I want," I tell him with sincerity.

Sniper

Her words fill me up and heat rolls through my body. My arms go around her and I pull her to me, the core of her pressed tightly to the front bulge of my jeans. My lips seek hers and when they touch, I can't get enough of her.

When she pulls away from me, I grasp on to her, not wanting to let her go.

"Wait," she tells me. Oh, this girl and her sassy mouth.

She takes off her shirt and her large breasts are barely covered in a black bra. She bends over, removing her jeans, and I sit here and watch as she slowly pulls them down her legs. When she stands up, her curvy body has my mouth watering and my hands itching to get a hold of her.

I reach out for her, but she backs away. Her hands go behind her back to unsnap her bra. She takes a deep breath, then lets it fall down her shoulders and to the floor. Holy fuck! I moan. The tips of her breasts are hard and right then and there I decide I've had enough of this. I have to touch her.

I stand up and she takes another step back. "Honey, quit backing away from me. I'll take you against the door, on the floor, or on the bed. You pick. But I'm getting in there one way or another."

"But, but, I had this whole lap dance planned out, and I've been practicing…"

My hands fist at my sides. "Lap dance? Who have you been practicing on?"

Her hands go up on her hips and she cocks her leg out. "What? No one. I've just been watching the women and practicing in here… by myself."

"Honey, fuck yeah, I will take it." I spot the chair in the corner of the room and move it to the center. I sit down in it and pull her to stand between my legs.

"Wait," she says and walks to the dresser and turns on some music on a cd player. As soon as it starts playing, she starts swinging her hips side to side. I watch her as she bends over, her ass right in my face. She brings her underwear down her legs and steps out of them. The view of her rounded ass makes me want to reach out for her, but she spreads her legs apart and her swollen, wet slit is staring back at me.

I grip her hips and bring her closer to me, just wanting a touch. But she stands up and turns to face me, shaking her finger side to side. "Uh, uh – no touching."

She puts her hand on my knees and arches her back, pressing her bare breasts against me before rounding her back and standing up again. The steady beat of the music floats in the air and her body is in perfect sync. She's teasing me and I adjust my hard cock in my jeans.

She tugs my shirt over my head, and she missteps at the sight of my naked torso. She walks around the back of the chair, caressing my shoulders and my back. When she comes to the front of me, she kicks her leg out and straddles my thigh, grinding her pussy into it.

"Fuck," I mutter. She doesn't stop. Her hips are gyrating against me and I can't take it anymore.

I pick her up and lay her on the bed. She looks up at me with wide eyes. "Did I do something wrong?"

"No, honey, you did everything right."

Her arms go around my neck. "I thought that's what you would want."

"The only thing I want right now is to be buried balls deep inside of you."

I pull off my boots, and then my jeans and underwear, before pulling her to the edge of the bed.

"I can't wait. I need to be inside you now," I tell her as I stroke my cock through her drenched heat.

"Yes," she moans.

I push into her all the way until I'm buried balls deep inside of her and I can feel her pussy clenching and vibrating around my dick.

Heaven. She feels like heaven. I kiss her lips, down her throat and suck on her nipples, all while I pound into her pussy. I lift her hips up and don't give up or slow down. I keep thrusting into her until she wraps her hand around my neck and pulls me in for a kiss. She backs away and looks me dead in the eye. I can't look away from her. Her face is taut and I can feel her pussy holding on to me with each drag of my hips. When I feel her pulse around me, I thrust even deeper until I'm deep in her womb and she's begging me for more.

"Don't stop, don't stop!" she begs.

As if I could even think about stopping. I know I've probably bruised her hips, I'm gripping her so tightly, but that doesn't stop me. She's still begging me for it and so I give it to her until she's clamped down on me and screaming my name. I come so hard that I fear I might pass out. Her channel is so tight, she's milking me and I shoot stream after stream of hot cum deep into her womb.

I lift her up the bed and lie down beside her, trying to catch my breath.

AVERY

WE HAD SEX ALL NIGHT LONG. HE ROLLED OVER toward me so many times, I lost count. I swear the last time, when he was spooning me and he took me from behind, I was exhausted and sore. But I couldn't tell him no. I didn't want to.

Now that it's morning, I snuggle farther into his hot, hard body. I lift my knee to wrap my leg around him and stop when he moans underneath me.

"Sorry. You're just so warm," I admit and burrow farther into him.

"Honey, we have to talk." His voice is husky and instantly, I get worried. I raise my head to look at him and I can see it in his face.

I sit up and wrap the sheet around myself, covering my bare breasts.

He puts his hand on the cover at my thigh. "You

44

don't have to worry about your husband anymore, Avery."

Instantly, my heart starts racing. I get up from the bed and start tugging on my clothes. "What do you mean? What did you do?"

He sits up in the bed and swings his legs to the floor. "Honey, I can't tell you that. All I can tell you is that he will never bother you again. You are free to live your life the way you want to. You never have to look over your shoulder again."

I sit down in the chair across the room with my head in my hands. "It can't be that easy."

"I would never put you in danger. I wouldn't lie to you either. It's done. You're free, Avery."

"Really?" I take a deep breath. "You promise?"

"I promise." He starts walking toward me but stops when someone pounds on his door.

"Pres. We need you out here."

Jeremy walks to the door and holds it open. He doesn't care that he's naked; that doesn't stop him. "What do you want? I'm a little busy," he demands. Thankfully, I can't see who it is and they can't see me.

"Brick, Rancher and Rider got jumped last night. Rancher's in the hospital."

Jeremy slams his fist into the wall by the door and I jump in my seat. In a deadly voice, he asks, "Are they okay? Who did it?"

"They'll be fine. We're still working on it."

"Okay, I'll be right there."

He shuts the door and turns toward me. "I have to take care of this. Stay here."

I get up from the chair. "Jeremy," I start but then I see the worry on his face. "Okay, yeah, I'll be here."

He bends over me and kisses me briefly before running out the door, leaving me to my thoughts.

Sniper

"WHAT THE FUCK do you mean we don't know who jumped them?" I demand of the room.

I called an emergency church and then sent Keeper to the hospital to pick up Rancher. Everyone is staring back at me, but no one is answering.

"Okay, what do we know about the bar they were at?"

Rider clears his throat. "It's not owned by any club, but I recognized them as members of the Kings. They had the Kings patch on their cuts."

"Finally, we're getting somewhere. What happened, Rider?"

Rider gets up and starts pacing the room. One of the reasons we call him Rider is he can't sit still. "Brother, we were there for the pussy. That's it. Just some bar. We were watching the show when we were attacked from behind. I think there were five of them, three on Brick and one each on Rancher and me. One of the waitresses had a baseball bat and helped get them off of Brick before we got out of there."

"A woman saved your asses?" I ask him incredulously. "Really, we're supposed to be badass bikers that save women, not the other way around."

Rider's face turns red. "Yeah, again, we were caught by surprise. We had no idea there would be trouble. Not like that."

"Where's the girl?" I hate to even ask, but if they left the girl behind, she's dead by now.

"Brick has her in his room, trying to calm her ass down. She didn't come willingly," Rider says, explaining Brick's absence.

"Fuck…. Okay, everyone, get your shit together. Smokey"—I turn to the vice president—"get a plan together. We will reconvene in two hours. Rancher should be back by then and maybe give us more intel. We don't lay down on this. Revenge is ours. Church is adjourned."

I start to walk out of the room and then turn back. "Come get me when Rancher gets here."

But I don't wait for an answer. I stalk out of the room and go back to find Avery.

I push open the door and walk in and about

double over at the sight before me. "Where the fuck do you think you're going?"

Avery whips around when I slam the door behind me. If this isn't all fucked up… "What were you going to do, sneak out of here?"

She turns back around and starts folding her clothes. "Of course not. I told you I would be here."

"Yeah, but for how long?" When she doesn't answer me, I crowd in next to her. "Where are you going?"

She wipes a tear from her cheek. What the fuck? I can't even deal with this right now. I don't usually handle women and emotions well. She turns toward me and in a small whisper, she says, "You said I was free."

Stunned, I look at her until it dawns on me. She thought I was getting rid of her, that I was giving her an out.

I turn her around and walk her over to the bed, pulling her down next to me. "You're free from your husband. That's all I meant. You're not free from me. You never will be. What I did was for you. I couldn't let him get away with treating you the way he did. I made sure he paid for it. I didn't want you looking over your shoulder for the rest of your life. But I have to be honest with you, I also did it for me. I needed you completely free from him, Avery. I needed you to be able to do whatever you wanted with your life. I only hoped that whatever you decided you want, you would choose to do it with me."

She stares at me the whole time I am talking, and the more I say the more serene her face becomes until when I'm finished there is nothing but hope shining in her eyes.

"You want me to stay?" she asks me.

I pull her up onto my lap and I don't even feel bad that she is going to feel my stiff rod pressed against her thigh. I don't know how many times I had her last night, but it wasn't enough. It will never be enough. "You don't have a choice, Avery. Not really. I can't give you up now. I never dreamed I would ever want to settle down, but when I skipped the bar last night because I didn't want to be away from you a minute longer, well, I knew then. I love you, Avery. I'll never want anyone else, not as long as I have you."

She throws herself at me and I catch her tight against me. Her face is buried in my neck and all I hear is muffled words. "What is it, honey?" I ask her.

She pulls back from me. "I love you too." And then she's kissing up my neck to my mouth. When our lips meet, I make it my mission that she never doubts how I feel about her again.

EPILOGUE

AVERY

I STAND BACK AND WATCH IT ALL UNFOLD. RANCHER got here and everyone has joined together in the main part of the club. He's on crutches and he is one pissed-off man.

However, not as pissed off as Madison, the woman that Brick brought home with him from the bar. They were arguing a few minutes ago, but now she has her back turned to him and she's ignoring everything that is being said.

I'm pretty sure I like her already.

Jeremy, or Sniper out here, is talking to everyone but he has his front pressed tightly to my back. If anyone is surprised by our relationship, they're not showing it.

His hands grip my hips and I swear I can feel the moisture pooling in my panties. He bends down and kisses my ear. He whispers to me, "Can you take Madison and find her some clothes to change into?"

I look over at her and she's still in her waitressing outfit from the night before. I tell him yes and start to walk away. He grabs on to my hand and pulls me in for another kiss. He tells me, "Don't be long. I need you again, honey. And soon."

I smile up at him and then walk across the room to where Madison and Brick are standing. "Hey, Brick. Hi, Madison. I'm Avery. Do you want to go with me so we can find you some clothes to change into?"

Brick stares between the two of us and I'm surprised when a growl escapes his lips. I look between the two of them and then smile up at him. "Easy, big guy. I'll bring her right back."

I watch as Madison looks up at him and then she follows me to my room that I share with Sniper.

Sniper

RANCHER IS out of the hospital and Smokey already has a plan to seek revenge. I talk to them for a few minutes, going over the details before I walk over to Brick because he's the one person I haven't gotten to talk to about all this.

"Everything okay, Brick?" I ask him.

"Fuck no, it's not okay," he grunts back at me. "A woman had to save my ass. I'm losing my touch," he admits.

We watch as Avery and Madison walk back in. Madison has changed out of her waitress uniform and as she walks across the room, her eyes are on Brick and no one else.

"Fuck, I'm in trouble, Pres." His husky voice almost sounds scared.

I look between him and Madison, and I voice my agreement. The poor man isn't going to know what hit him.

Avery walks up to me and throws her arms around my waist, then raises on her tiptoes to kiss my cheek. "You ready to turn in, Sniper?"

I smile down at her. "Yeah, honey, let's go."

I wrap my arm around her proudly, tell Brick and Madison good night, and I take my woman back to my – our - room. "How about another lap dance, honey?"

She laughs, but as soon as we walk in the room, she turns on the music, drowning out the party in the other room, and shimmies her body back into my arms – right where she belongs.

Keep Reading for Brick's story.

BRICK

1

BRICK

She's standing over a downed man with a baseball bat in her hand. Her chest is heaving from the exertion and I should probably be pissed right now. Hell, I should probably be helping my brothers that are still fighting. But instead, I'm turned on as fuck.

She has on the waitress uniform for the Back Roads Bar. A pair of black shorts and tight black T-shirt that is knotted at her waist showing off her larger curves. I had noticed her as soon as we walked in and made sure to sit in her section. I'm not the only one that noticed her. Her long blond hair, curvy body and innocent look has my brothers watching her too.

She walked up to our table. "What can I get you?" Her eyes move around the table, but they keep coming back to me.

"Are you going to be dancing tonight?" Rider asks her with a grin. He glances over to the stage where a woman is pole dancing.

"No, I don't dance, but I'll get your beers for you." She smiles at him.

I growl and don't even realize I'm doing it until everyone at the table turns to me, including her. I must have been loud if they heard me over the blaring music. I don't want her smiling at Rider. Hell, I don't want her to smile at anyone but me. "Give her a break, Rider. We'll take three beers."

She stands there looking at me for a minute and then realizes she's staring and turns around, rushing back to the bar.

"Dibs," I tell Rancher and Rider as I watch her fine ass walk away.

"Technically, I talked to her first… rules are rules, brother." Rider claps his hands and rubs them together. He's crazy if he thinks I'm going to just let him make her one of his one-night stands. Just one look at her tells me there's something special about her. I watch her across the room and she's waiting on the bartender to give her the beers. She looks back at our table and I smile at her. Her lips lift on the ends and she looks away quickly.

I look over at Rider and he's already lost interest in the waitress and is eyeing the dancers. Rancher is doing something on his phone.

When I look her way again she's walking back

toward us. She has a nervousness about her but she still smiles at me. Before she approaches the table, her face goes from a smile to fear and her eyes widen. I don't have time to process what's happening before Rancher, Rider and I are jerked from our seats.

I don't even get a good look at my attackers before they try to take me down from behind. Whoever it is knows us… knows me. There are two men holding me and a third beating me. My body jerks with every punch. I struggle, trying to fight them all off. My brothers are in their own battles and I see the waitress start to walk toward us. "No!" I scream at her and she stops.

I fight and jerk my arms, but even me, the sergeant of arms of the Exiled Guardians, the strongest fucker of the club, I can't break free. I jerk my hands trying to free myself, but I can't, no matter how hard I pull.

All of a sudden I hear a loud crunch and the man in front of me jerks his head and falls to the ground. Only when he falls do I see that my girl, hell the girl I still don't know the name of, has a baseball bat over her head, staring at the fallen man. One of the men holding me releases my arm to go toward her and it's then that I get the upper hand. I take down both men easily, not wasting any time to get over to her.

"Are you okay?" I ask her and watch as she

stares open mouthed at the man face down on the floor, bleeding from his head. It's then that I see the name on his cut, Fallen Kings, rivals to the Exiled Guardians.

She doesn't answer me. She's staring at the man and I want to explain to her that head wounds bleed more than normal and that he'll be okay. I'm sure she's not used to violence, at least not where she gets involved. When she still doesn't look at me or respond, I throw her over my shoulder and carry her over behind the bar.

When I put her down, she is still trying to look around me. "Stay here. I'll be right back."

All the people in the bar are watching us. Most bar fights, people jump in. Well, not when two rival clubs are going at it. People tend to stay out of our way.

Rancher is on the ground, bleeding from his leg. Rider now is fighting two men, the one that pulled him out of his chair and the one that got Rancher.

I jump in, ready for this to be over, ready to get me and her out of here. I pull one of the men off Rider and punch him, causing him to fall back on the bar and to the ground. I look at her one more time and when I turn around, Rider has taken out the other one and put him on the floor.

"Rider, help him." I point over at Rancher, who's lifting himself off the floor. I go back to her and she seems to have gotten herself together but she's still looking at the man she hit.

"Do you have a purse or anything you want to take with you?" I ask her.

She shakes her head. "What?"

Putting my hands on her shoulders, I ask her again, "Honey, we probably only have a minute to get out of here before the cops pull in with sirens blaring. Where's your purse?"

The bartender sets it on the bar beside her. She grabs it and starts to walk, but stops herself. "Wait, I'm not going anywhere."

I shake my head. "What's your name?"

"Madison," she whispers to me huskily.

"Madison, you just took down a Fallen King. They are not going to forget this. You need to come with me so I can protect you." I grab her hand and pull her after me.

"No, I'll just explain…" she starts.

But what she doesn't realize is that there is no explaining when it comes to the Kings. My heart starts racing, not from the exertion, but from thinking about what they'll do to her if they find her.

A woman, a friend of hers I'm guessing, in the same uniform walks up to her. "Madison, he's right. You better go."

I don't wait for her to respond. I lift Madison

over my shoulder once again and stride out of the bar with her hanging over me. I expected some kind of fight, but there isn't one. Maybe it's finally hit her... she can't stay here.

2

MADISON

When we get outside, he sets me on my feet and puts my purse into a compartment on his bike.

"What about you?" I ask him as he grabs a helmet, putting it on my head and snapping it under my chin.

He smirks at me. "I'm fine."

He looks over at the other two bikers, nodding his head at them. They look at me, but they don't seem to question what he's doing bringing me along. He straddles the bike and holds his hand out to me.

"I've never ridden on a bike before," I tell him.

"That's okay. I've never had a woman on the back of my bike before."

I feel that him saying that to me is telling me something, maybe something profound. I've heard about bikers and having women on their bikes. It's supposed to be special to some of them. I wonder if it's the case with him. I put my hand in his to help me balance as I throw my leg over the bike. Once I'm settled, he reaches back and grips my thighs, pulling me closer to him. When the front of my body is snug against his back, he hollers back at me, "Lean when I lean."

He grabs my hands and pulls them around him, holding them to him until I grip on to his hard abs. He starts the motor, and I squeeze him, trying to get his attention. "Hey, what's your name?"

"Brick. Hold on."

He pulls out of the parking lot and I grip on to him even tighter.

When I came into work tonight, I never dreamed this was how my night would go. I thought it would be like every other night. Yes, I've seen a bar fight before. But never like the one I saw tonight. And I've definitely never jumped into the middle of one.

But I noticed Brick the second he walked into the door of the Back Roads Bar. Admittedly, he's hard not to notice. When you have three bikers the size of him and his friends, you sort of take notice. But there was something else. It was almost like I couldn't look away from him.

Which is weird for me honestly. I'm not that girl. The one that fawns over a man. Of course, it could be that I haven't had time to notice one. Not in a while, anyway. Growing up, it was just my mom and me. She worked all the time, but she also made sure I always had everything I needed. I graduated high school and was in my 3rd year of college when my life fell apart. My mother, after a long battle with cancer, passed away. I dropped out of school and came to work at the bar. It was the only well-paying job I could find in this small town.

So gone was my free-living, happy go lucky life. My boyfriend broke up with me and I pretty much lost touch with all my friends. But I was surviving… at least the best way I knew how.

I've had my head laid against Brick's back and I finally lift it and look over his shoulder. We're flying down the empty road, only us and the two other bikes in sight. It doesn't seem long before we are pulling off onto a gravel road and driving into a facility where a number of bikes are parked outside. We get waved through the gate and as soon as Brick parks, he stands up and helps me off.

One of the bikers gets off his bike and helps the other. It's obvious the other man doesn't want the help, but he's accepting it anyway, since he seems to be hurt pretty bad. "Brick, man, I'm going to grab my cage and take Rancher to the hospital."

"Call Doc, have him come here," Brick tells him.

"I've tried texting and calling him. No answer," he responds.

He walks over to a car and helps the one they call Rancher into the passenger seat. "I'll let you know," he hollers to us before getting in and pulling out of the gravel lot.

I watch them leave and then turn to Brick to find him staring at me. "So, uh, where am I at and can you take me home?"

"You can't go home... not until I know you'll be safe."

I take a deep breath and slowly let it out. I hate change and don't handle it well. I should be more upset about all of this, but a part of me maybe feels better about the excitement of it all. I've spent every day this past year working and sleeping. "So where am I at?"

"The Exiled Guardians' clubhouse. Or my second home." His chest puffs out and I can hear the pride in his voice when he says it.

I wrap my arms around me, hugging myself. "So they were bikers... and you wouldn't let me stay there. But you brought me to a whole club-house of bikers?"

"Princess, you didn't beat one of us in the head with a baseball bat."

I cringe at his words. He's right; I did. I still don't fully understand what made me jump in.

He's looking at me as if he's trying to under-stand me. I want to tell him, *Good luck, I don't even understand me half the time.*

He cocks his head to the side. "You saved me back there. I owe you."

His words should make me feel better, but they only put a pit in my stomach. I'll admit it, at one time when I was on the back of his bike, I imagined that I was his girlfriend. The fact that he's helping me because he owes me doesn't really fit in with the dream I was having.

"I've taken care of myself for a long time, Brick. I'd like to go home… please."

"No," he answers immediately and starts walking toward the door of his clubhouse.

I grab his shoulder and pull him around to face me. "What do you mean, 'no'? I want to go home. You're not my keeper. You're helping me because you feel like you owe me. Well, you don't owe me anything. I expunge your debt to me. Anything that happens to me will not be on your head. So please, will you take me home?"

3

BRICK

I SEE THE FRUSTRATION ON HER FACE AND THE WAY she's all riled up has me thinking things that I've never thought before. I swear at one point, in the middle of the fucking bar fight, I was picturing her pregnant with my babies. And when she was on the back of my bike with her thighs gripping me, well, I wanted to pull over and take her right then. It's like a punch to the stomach thinking about it. Especially with the life I live. I never thought I would want to settle down. But hell, in this moment with her, even though she's a little pissed off at me right now, well, I can picture it in my mind and I want it. I want it bad.

I fist my hands at my sides. If I don't, I'm going to touch her. And if I touch her, I'm afraid there's no stopping me then. "I can't take you back."

Most people don't question me. I say something

and they agree. That's not the case with her. "What do you mean you can't take me back?"

I shake my head, and with nostrils flaring, I turn her until her back is pressed against the building. I can hear the steady thump of the party going on inside. There are bikers, my brothers, standing by their bikes talking not too far from us. But I tune all of that out. I press my body against hers and look down at her. How do I tell her I want her? How do I tell her it's not just for one night, when that's all I've ever known.

"I can't take you back, Madison. Physically, I can't take you back there. I don't know why... I can't explain it. All I can tell you is that I can't let you out of my sight. I can't risk you getting hurt."

She's looking back at me and her face softens. I still don't think she completely understands. I don't think she gets the importance that she's the only woman that I've ever allowed on the back of my bike.

After we stare back at each other for I don't know how long and I think that any second I'm going to kiss her, she finally lifts her shoulders in a shrug. "Okay."

"Okay?" I question her. That was too easy.

"I'll stay tonight. But I have to go to work tomorrow. If I don't, they'll give my job to someone else, and I can't lose my job." She walks away from me and stands by the door to go into the clubhouse.

Damn, I wish I could take her to my house. But with the attack, the clubhouse is the safest place for tonight. I walk over to her and wonder if I should warn her about what she's about to see. I decide not to, and open the door, letting her even further into my life.

We stop when we walk in. I expect her to gasp, to look outraged, pissed off or even upset that I've brought her here. But she's not. She looks around the room and her gaze doesn't even slow down when she sees one of the brothers and two of the sweet butts making out in the corner. When she gets around the room, she looks up at me. "I'm not feeling up for a party. Where am I sleeping?"

I grab her hand and walk her past everyone toward my room. A few of the men holler at me, trying to wave me over, but I just nod at them and keep walking. I spot Smokey, the vice president, and ask him, "Where's Pres?"

"He's in his room. I wouldn't bother him." He gives me a look telling me that he's not alone.

"Okay. Church. Early in the morning. Get rid of the sweet butts and call everyone in. Have the prospects at the door. Send a few to the hospital to keep an eye on Rider and Rancher, they are there. Rancher's hurt, but nothing serious," I tell him.

He starts to ask me something, but with one look at Madison, he changes his mind and merely nods.

I hear the music stop before I get to my room.

I didn't even introduce Madison to him. I'm glad she didn't want to hang out, because brothers

or not, I don't want to hang in a room with her and them until they understand they are to leave her alone.

I open the door to my room and usher her in. She looks around the bare walls. "This is where you live? Do all of you live here?"

I try to look at it through her eyes and I see the bare walls, with nothing personal to be seen anywhere. "When I stay at the club, this is my room. I have a house just down the road."

"And you brought me to your club instead of your house." She hugs herself and looks down at the ground. "Look, Brick, if you have a girlfriend or wife at home waiting on you, I don't think I need to be staying in your room. Plus, uh, I don't know what you think about me, but"—she points at the bed—"I'm not sleeping with you."

I shake my head. She doesn't get it, but how can I expect her to? She just met me and honestly, I'm surprising myself here. Any other woman I would have already been balls deep in by the door so as to not dirty up my bed. I would have had her out of my room and back at the party. But that's not even entered my mind with Madison. Well, I've thought about fucking her, that's no doubt. But I'm trying to figure out how to keep her in my bed instead of out of it.

"No wife. No girlfriend. I brought you here because we just got into a brawl with our rivals and until we know how they plan to retaliate or what we plan to do… Hell, woman, that's club business, anyway. Until I know you will be safe at my house, we are here."

I swear it's only been a few hours and she's already got me talking about more stuff than I should be talking about with her.

She points at the bed and before she even gets started, I tell her honestly, "The bed's clean. I'm the only one that's slept in it for a while. I will bunk with one of my brothers, but only if you promise me that you stay in this room unless I come and get you."

She nods her head at me and it's only then that I realize I've been holding my breath waiting on her to agree. I don't know why I'm so worried. If I tell a prospect, he wouldn't let her leave. I realize now that I want her to want to stay.

Fuck, my mind's fucked up right now.

I start to walk out of the room, only because it's killing me to stand next to her like this. I need a few minutes to myself. I need to figure out where my head's at.

"Wait, where are you going?" she asks me.

I turn back around to face her. "To find a room."

She sits down on the edge of the bed. "Do you think I killed him?"

It's on the tip of my tongue to tell her I fucking hope so, but I stop when I see the sadness on her face. I sit down next to her. "No, I think he'll be fine."

"Do you think he will really come and find me? You know… for revenge."

When she raises her head, I can see the fear in her eyes. Yes, I know him or his club will not let

this go. Something will come of it, but she doesn't need to know all the gory details. "You saved me back there, Madison. I know you ain't used to this kind of life, but doing that, helping me back there, well, it may make me look like a pussy, but it puts you under club protection. No one is going to mess with you."

She nods her head at me. I can tell by her face that she doubts my words. I would give anything to convince her she's safe.

I stand up and walk over to the dresser, pulling out one of my shirts. "Here you go, sleep in this. We'll figure out more clothes tomorrow."

She takes it from me and lays it on the bed next to her and reaches for the hem of the shirt she's wearing. She starts to tug it up and like a man starving with a steak in front of him, I start to drool.

She stops mid motion and points to the wall. "Can you turn around?"

Reluctantly I face the wall, and the sound of clothes coming off has me itching to turn around. If I was any less of a man, I would ignore her request and watch her, but I won't do that to her. I want her to trust me.

"Okay, I'm good," she calls out.

I turn around and she's folding her clothes before walking over to set them on the dresser. I watch her ass shake under my shirt and my cock stiffens in my pants. *I have to get the fuck out of here.*

"Where are you going?" she asks me when I have my hand on the knob.

I don't even turn around, just lean my head against the closed door. "I was going to let you get some sleep."

I can hear her take a deep breath and slowly let it out. "Will you stay with me… just a little longer?"

I can hear the need in her voice. I lift my head and nod, turning around. "Sure. Go ahead, get into bed."

I watch her ass as she climbs into my bed and burrows under my covers. I imagine if I was in the bed with her we wouldn't need the covers. The bed would be scorching.

I flip the light off and walk over to the other side of the room. I tug my boots off and lean back in the chair.

"What got you here, Brick? Why a motorcycle club?" she asks me in the darkness.

I expect to hear judgment in her question, but I can't hear it. All I hear is curiosity.

"I was in the army. Our president, my brother Sniper, was in too. We saw so much while we were there." I take a deep breath. "When we got out, we had trouble adjusting to everyday life. We started the club together. We bought a few businesses in town, and before we knew it, there were other men, ones that had the same moral code as us, but couldn't adjust to their lives like before. We built this brotherhood. They may not be my real brothers, but to me they are."

My voice is husky as I talk about it. I never talk about my time in the service or my problems adjusting afterwards. I usually just ignore it when people ask me.

4

MADISON

"That's amazing, Brick," I tell him honestly.

"Why?" he mutters.

The darkness makes me feel safe, more open to talk. "Because you made your own family. One that accepts you for who you are, one that stands by you. Not everyone has that." My voice is thick with emotion.

"What about you, Madison? Why are you working at a bar? Do you have someone at home that will be worried about you?"

I roll to my side and look over at him. All I can see is his outline; I can't see his face. "I don't have anyone. Not really. My mom died last year, and it was only me and her. I guess that's why I think what you're doing here is amazing. And well, I work at the bar because it was the best paying job I could find in town. After Mom passed, I quit college and have been working since."

He leans forward in the chair and puts his elbows on his knees. His face is now lighted by the moon shining in from the window. The pity in his expression is almost too much for me to bear. I get it all the time, anytime someone hears my story. But I don't want pity. Not now, and not from him.

"Well, you're not alone now. You have a club of brothers that would lay their lives down for you. Without question."

"Is that really how this works? So you're my 'brother' now?" I ask him quietly, waiting for his response.

He cracks his knuckles and then brings them together. "Yes, that's honestly how this works, without question. However, I feel like I need to tell you that nothing I'm feeling toward you is brotherly."

I try to fight it, but I can't stop it. A smile forms on my lips and I hope that he can't see it in the darkness. "Okay." I roll back over onto my back. "Good night, Brick."

He sighs. "Good night, princess."

"Hey, Brick?"

"Yeah?" He settles further into the chair.

"What's your real name… or is Brick your real name?" I ask him. Not that Brick doesn't suit him. It definitely does.

"Ben. My birth name is Ben."

I turn my head toward him. "Ben. Can I call you that?"

He seems to think about it for a minute and then finally agrees. "In here, or when it's just the two of us, you can call me Ben. When we're out there, with my brothers, I need you to call me Brick."

I quietly tell him okay. "Hey, uh, how old are you?"

He chuckles and the deepness of it vibrates in the room. "I'm thirty-two. Is that too old for you, princess?"

I stutter, but answer him honestly, "No, I wasn't asking because of that. I was just wondering."

"How old are you?"

I put my hands behind my head and look up at the ceiling. "I'll be twenty-two next month."

"So I'm ten years older than you. Does that bother you?"

I tilt my head to the side to look at him and wish I could see his face. "Why would it bother me? I'm leaving here tomorrow, Ben."

"Keep thinking that, princess."

Frustrated, I throw my hands into the air. "Why do you keep calling me that? I don't act like a princess. I'm actually one of the least high mainte-nance women I know."

His answer is gruff. "I don't mean anything by

it. It's just a reminder to myself that you're differ-ent. More different than any woman I've ever met. You deserve to be treated better than how I usually treat a woman."

I'm surprised by his answer. I thought for sure he was calling me that for another reason. I lift up on my elbow. "How do you normally treat women?"

I'm skeptical even as I ask him. The way he's treated me has been like a pure gentleman. I can't imagine him treating a woman poorly.

"Let's just say, women have only served one purpose for me. And I don't lie to them about it. They know from the get-go where they stand."

"And I'm different?" I ask him, surprised by his answer.

"You're definitely different."

"Well, I've never known a princess to beat a man over a head with a baseball bat. I'm just sayin'." I huff at him and turn over. I don't realize it until it comes out of my mouth that I'm practically begging him to treat me like one of his other women, a one-night stand. I bite my lip and roll my eyes.

"Good night, princess."

"Night," I mutter.

Brick

Hours later, I'm stuck in a nightmare of my own, but the screams this time are different. It's not the voices of my comrades, but the voice of Madison.

I jolt awake and about fall to the ground when I jump out of the chair. "Madison, Madison," I say to her while I try to wake her up.

The initial scream has turned into cries and I frantically try to wake her up. When her eyes finally open they're wide, and I see fear in their depths.

"It's okay, honey. I'm here. You're okay. No one is going to hurt you," I tell her. I sit down on the bed next to her and stroke her head.

She staring at me, and I hope I'm not scaring her even more.

"Brick, will you lay down with me?" she asks me.

And even though I know it's not a good idea, I still can't refuse her. She scoots over and I lie down beside her. She's lying in the crook of my arm and I feather my fingers through her hair. "Are you okay?" I ask her.

She nods her head, but doesn't say anything.

Her hand slides up my belly and rests on my chest. Her finger slides in circles and I bite back the moan that is about to escape from my lips.

Instinctively, I reach up and wrap my hand around hers, stopping the movement. "Princess, I watched you sleep for a few hours. I made myself stay out of your bed. But you're pushing it now."

She raises her head and looks at me. "What if I don't want you to hold back? What if I told you that I'm fine with you treating me like you treat those other women... I mean, a one-night stand is all I have to give."

I stroke my hand down her back and squeeze her ass, pulling her against my hip. Her shirt, or I guess I should say my shirt, has ridden up and her panty-clad cheek in my hand is everything. "There's no way. You're not like any other woman. But I do want you, and I'll take you tonight, tomorrow and the night after."

She shrugs her shoulders. "I'm leaving, Brick. I have to go back to my life. Please, give me tonight."

An inner battle rages inside me. I won't turn her down, I can't. But there's no way I will have her and let her go. One night with her and she's tied to me for eternity. I know it and have no doubts about it.

Instead of answering her, I lean my head down and capture her lips with mine. The kiss goes from soft and timid to deep and thorough in a matter of seconds. Our tongues duel with each other and I stroke mine through her mouth, tasting her sweetness.

She climbs up on me then and when I feel her soft curvy body on top of mine, I wrap my arms around her to hold her to me.

She pulls away and tugs at my shirt. "You have too many clothes on."

"So do you," I tell her and pull her shirt up and off her body. Her large breasts are pressed against me and I want to feel her skin more than anything I've ever wanted in my life. Clad only in panties, she grinds her pussy into the hardness between my legs and I grip her hips, grinding my cock against her.

She's kissing my neck, my ear and across my lips. "Clothes, Ben, I need your clothes off," she begs me and tries to pull my shirt off. I lean up to help her and as soon as I'm shirtless underneath her, I reach between us and undo my jeans. Her hands are stroking my chest, each muscle flexing under her touch. I lift her under the arms and pull her up my body until she's straddling my stomach. I lean up and finish undoing my jeans before pulling them and my underwear down my legs, then kicking them off with my feet. Would it have been easier to get up and take them off? Abso-fuckin-lutely. But then I would have had to move away from her, and I don't plan on doing that anytime soon.

I'm huffing from fighting with my pants and she's just smiling down at me. I reach up and tweak her hard nipple. "Something funny, princess?"

She shakes her head side to side, and I watch as her breasts jiggle with the movement. I cup her then, feeling their weight in my hands and massaging them while she throws her head back in ecstasy.

Pulling her down to me, I alternate suckling them until she's grinding into me and playing with her breasts is no longer enough.

"Panties. Panties off. You take them off, or I rip them off," I tell her as I nuzzle against her cleavage.

She slides them down her hips and tries to take them off, but can't.

"They're coming off, princess," I tell her right before I grip one side and rip it and then move to the other side and rip it. I pull the cloth from between her legs and I can't resist bringing it to my nose and inhaling her scent.

"Ben!" she exclaims and tries to take it from me. "What?"

"Those are the only pair of underwear I have with me," she explains.

"That's okay. I'll get you more, but honestly, I'm fine without you wearing them. Then I can have you anytime I feel the urge." I smile at her.

She just shakes her head. She reaches behind herself and feels around until she has her hand wrapped around my girth. "What the…?"

She lifts up and moves backwards to my legs so that my cock is standing straight up in front of her. "No way, there's no way." She's staring at my cock and I swear it twitches at her.

Instead of answering her, I reach down between

her legs, and the sweet cream of her pussy coats my fingers. "Someone's ready." I stroke her with my fingers, entering her slowly, first one finger, then two, trying to stretch her so she can at least enjoy it when I take her. When she starts riding my hand, I flash my fingers across her swollen clit and she releases a groan like nothing I've ever heard before from the back of her throat, and it doesn't stop. I increase the pressure and when I feel her body tighten and her nub swell, I stroke her back and forth until she's coming and her juices are coating my hand.

I bring my fingers to my lips and lick her flavor off of them, moaning at her taste.

Her chest is heaving, and before she comes completely down from her high, I pull her up until I'm lined up at her entrance. Thoughts of condoms barely register with me before the same image I had earlier, of her pregnant with our babies, lands in my mind. I slowly start to enter her and her hips tighten around mine. I lean up then to kiss her.

With each nip of my lips, I go deeper inside of her. Her hand is stroking my chest and when it caresses my nipple, I grip her hips and pull her down until she's fully seated on my cock. Her head drops and she moans into my mouth. I lay back on the pillow and look at her over top of me. Just looking at her full, curvy body has me hardening inside of her.

I drive up into her, gripping her hips, moving her up and down. Her slick, wet heat is wrapped around me and with every thrust, I feel her pussy vibrating around me. When her hips start moving quicker and her moans get louder, I pick up the pace, meeting her thrust for thrust. "Yes, princess, yes. Come all over my cock," I tell her.

Her body locks up over top of me and with one last thrust, I fill her full of cum. Her pussy sucks me in, milking me until I'm gasping for breath.

She falls down on top of me and when she starts to move, I put my hands on her ass, keeping her right where she's at. Right where she belongs.

I lazily move inside her, in my mind, giving her the last drop of cum.

"How about a shower?" I ask her with a pat to her ass.

She hesitates briefly. "Sure."

I help her off of me and then stand up next to her. I pick her up and her legs tighten around my waist. "Ben, I think I can walk."

I nuzzle her neck. "I know, but I like it better like this."

I walk with her to the bathroom and don't set her down until the water is heated up. I let her step into the shower first and I follow behind her.

I clean her and then myself before taking her again against the shower wall. I'm a man possessed, wanting to show her how good it can be between us, and wanting to claim her until she has no doubt that she's mine.

I'm relentless, taking her so many times throughout the night that she finally passes out from exhaustion. Then I wrap my body around hers and hold on tightly through the night.

5

MADISON

WHEN LIGHT COMES THROUGH THE WINDOW, I TURN my head and bury myself deeper into the warmth. My first thought is the feeling of soreness from my body. Even though I'm merely lying here, I can feel my muscles tightening.

My second thought is that I haven't felt 'safe' and protected like this in a long time. I rest my head down on Ben's chest, feeling the steady dip and rise of his breathing and gentle thump of his heartbeat under my cheek.

I think back to last night and all the ways he took me. My body has never been worshipped like he did last night. He made me feel confident. How could I not be, when just looking at my naked body had him losing all control?

I clench my eyes together. *I have to go*, I think to myself. Nothing good can come of this. I have to work and although it seems that he and his club have their own beef with the Kings, the men from last night, I can't risk him getting hurt to save me. *No, I need to go*. I need to get out of here before my heart gets any more involved.

A knock on the door, and someone bellowing "Church" is how Ben wakes up. He instantly jerks awake and gets out of bed, looking for his pants.

I've read enough motorcycle romance books to know what church is. As he's getting dressed, he leans over and kisses me. "Mornin', princess. Stay here and as soon as church is over, I'll get you something to eat."

I reach over the side of the bed and spot his shirt I was wearing last night. I reach for it and then tug it over my head. I need to be clothed, because I know we are about to have a disagreement. Unfortunately, it's one that I am going to have to win.

I stand up from the bed and even though I have no underwear on or any to put on, I still feel better not standing here naked.

"I'm fine, Ben. I'm going to go. I have to work tonight." I start pulling on my shorts from the night before.

"You're not leaving." He raises up to his full height.

I grab my bra and start to put it on. He's staring at me and I point to the wall for him to turn around.

He doesn't turn away. Instead, he takes a step toward me. "I've already seen you, princess. You going to hide from me now?"

I take a step back and raise his shirt over my head. I start putting my bra on. "I already explained this to you. I have to keep my job."

"Fuck that job. You're not going back there," he demands.

My mouth drops open and my eyes widen. "What do you mean, I'm not going back there? What do you want me to do? There's nothing else that pays anywhere close to what I make there. I can't live without it. No thanks, I'm keeping my job."

He gets a fierce look on his face but we are interrupted when someone hollers through the door again, "Brick, church, man!"

"Start without me," he bellows.

I shrink back away from him, because the mean voice I just heard is not the Ben I know.

He watches me as I step back away from him. He holds his hands up in front of him, palms facing me. "I would never hurt you. I would never let anyone hurt you. I thought you would have figured it out last night, but if not, then I'm doing something wrong. I want you here… with me. Not just tonight, not tomorrow. Forever."

Hope flares in my chest, but just as quickly I tamp it down. "No, Ben. I won't stay here and have you getting hurt trying to defend me. I can take care of myself. I've done it a long time."

He puts his hands on my shoulders and I can feel myself weakening. His touch controls me. "Really, is this what this is about? You're worried about me? Honey, I know you may not have faith in me after seeing me last night. But I am the sergeant of arms for the club. I had three men on me at one time, and I was sidetracked. They got me, fuck, all of us from behind. But I can take care of myself. I can take care of you."

I don't say anything. I want to. I want to tell him okay and I will never leave his side. But that's not really realistic. Who really has forever after only knowing someone for one day? "I can't just quit my job."

He leans down and kisses me, completely making me forget my train of thought. "Look, until I know you're safe, I can't let you—" When he sees my eyebrows raise at the word 'let,' he wraps his hand around the back of my neck. "I mean, I want you safe. I need you safe. Trust me to take care of this. Stay with me until it's over and then if you still want to leave, I'll take you home myself."

He doesn't wait for a response; he bends down and reaches under my shirt to cup my mound. I'm swollen and sore from last night, but I can still feel the pull in my lower belly from his touch. His finger slides through my slit and my head falls backward.

He kisses my exposed neck and when I moan, he lifts me up in his arms and carries me to the bed.

He lays me down and covers my body with his.

"I thought you had church?" I ask him.

"I do, but I have something more pressing that needs my attention right now," he whispers against my ear. I lie underneath of him while he pushes my body to its very limit of satisfaction.

6

BRICK

I KEEP MADISON SO BUSY, LOVING HER BODY, THAT I hope she has forgotten that she wants to leave. Just the mention of it had me ready to tear things apart.

After our lovemaking and another shower, we make it to the main room. I fix her a plate of food and we sit at the bar talking.

Everyone has gotten a good laugh about her saving me, but I just laugh right along with them. Her saving me was the best thing that ever happened to me.

I have my hand on her thigh as I'm talking to the guys.

"So, Rancher, you okay?"

"Yeah, I'm fine. Everything but my pride anyway. They cleaned out my stab wound and stitched me up. I'll be on crutches for a while. I tore something in my leg and they want me to go to physical therapy." He says it with disgust in his voice and immediately, I know that Rancher is not going to go to physical therapy. No matter how bad it hurts.

We talk a little about the night before and it isn't long before he walks away from me. I can tell how pissed off he is and I don't blame him. I only question which he's more pissed about: not being able to ride his bike or his horse.

Madison's phone rings in her pocket, and she digs it out and looks at the screen. I notice the name "Brent" on the caller ID. My hand tightens on her thigh. "It's my boss."

She had tried calling him earlier and he is just now returning her call.

"Hey Brent, I'm sorry I can't make it in tonight," she apologizes.

There's a brief silence and then, "What do you mean I'm fired?"

She looks at me with her eyes wide and then drops off the stool and walks over to the corner of the room. I hear her say, "It's not my fault they were in there trying to destroy your bar."

She's quiet for a long time, until she finally tells him, "Yeah, okay, I understand." And hangs up.

I walk up to her. "What was that about?"

"Apparently, I'm fired. He thinks it's better for him that I'm not there, ya know, to give the Kings a reason to come back." She's barely holding the tears back.

"Church!" one of the brothers hollers out.

Madison throws her hands out to the side. "How many times do y'all have church in a day?"

I smile at her and lace my fingers with hers. "C'mon, I'll take you back to the room."

On the way there, I stop one of the prospects. "Did you get what I needed?"

"Yep." He reaches into the bag on his shoulder and hands it to me.

"Thanks," I tell him and start walking toward the room.

As soon as I get her inside, I kiss her quickly. "I can't miss church again. I know you're upset about your job, but I don't want you to worry about it. We'll work it out. Here."

I hand her the envelope that the prospect just gave me.

"What's this?" she asks me, taking it from me.

"Open it."

She peels back the tab and opens it, pulling out its contents. "It's the college guide and application for the university."

"I know, and maybe you want to go somewhere else, maybe something online, but I thought this would give you at least something to look at while I'm busy."

She tries to give it back to me. "Why, Ben? I can't afford this."

"You want to graduate college, or at least I thought that's what you wanted. Think about it. Whatever you decide, I'm fine with." I kiss her and start to walk toward the door and turn around quickly. "Well, except for leaving me. That I'm not fine with."

I smile at her and walk out. I wanted to tell her not to leave, but I'm not even going to worry about it. I put a prospect at my door and told them if she leaves to come get me.

"In church?" he asks me.

Usually, prospects are not allowed to enter church, but I'm fucking making an exception on this.

"Yes," I assure him and go meet my brothers.

Madison

I LOOK DOWN at the papers in my hand, still not understanding what just happened. *Did he just say he would pay to send me to college?*

I sit down cross-legged on the bed and open the folders. I don't know how long I sit there, but the more I read, the more excited I get. Hours must have gone by because my stomach starts to growl. I sit up, slide my shoes on and open the door. There's a big, burly biker standing there.

"Hello?"

"Hey!" He nods his head and blocks my path.

"Uh, I need to get by," I tell him.

He shrugs his shoulders like it's no big deal, but I can see something in his eyes, maybe fear. "Where do you need to go?"

"To get something to eat. Maybe stretch my legs. Not that it's any of your business," I tell him before sliding beside him and walking down the hallway.

"Fine, I'll go get Brick from church. He's not going to like it." He walks behind me into the kitchen.

I get two slices of bread from the loaf and lay them down on the plate. I start spreading peanut butter on it and then look up at the prospect. "Why would you disturb the meeting because I'm going to the kitchen?"

"Because Brick told me to tell him if you moved. Will you stay here until I go get him?" he asks and I laugh. *Really, guys, I'm a grown woman.*

Brick walks into the kitchen and pats the man on the back. "It's okay, I got her."

I try not to let him see me laugh, because obviously the man was worried about interrupting church. He nods at Brick and backs out of the room.

I smile at Brick. "You got me, huh?"

"Yep, I definitely got you." He acts like he's going to kiss me and then at the last minute, takes a bite of my sandwich.

I swat him on the chest and start laughing. "Hey!"

He then kisses me and leans against the counter.

I hold up the jar of peanut butter. "Do you want me to make you one?"

He reaches for the bread and pulls out two slices. We work together to make his sandwich. I watch him take a few bites and try to concentrate on my food instead of his lips, or his body.

He takes another bite. "So what did you think of the school?"

"It's nice. But I'm not going to let you pay for me to go to school. I was thinking that maybe I can get a job around here. The commute will only be around twenty minutes." I take the last bite of my sandwich and wipe my mouth off.

He sets his food down and crosses his arms over his chest. "It will be hard to work and go to school full time. But ya know, while I was in church, I was thinking. If you're pregnant, you may want to consider going to school online."

He's looking at me with a smug look on his face. My brain starts working overtime, thinking about last night and how we didn't use protection, not once, and then I start trying to calculate the time since my last period. The whole time he's just smiling at me, as happy as he can be and not a care in the world.

Speechless, I don't even know what to say. He takes the last few bites of his sandwich and grips my hand. I think he planned to take me back to his room, but he stops once we get to the main room.

When I came through here earlier, there was no one. Now the room is filled and there are people everywhere. He grips my hips and puts me up on a bar stool. The conversation goes on around us and finally, I turn to him.

"You want me to get pregnant," I accuse him.

He smiles. "Yes."

I start stuttering. "You met me yesterday. How do you make that decision in one day? I could be a terrible mom. You don't know." I shake my head. "Wait, why are we even talking about this? I'm not pregnant. I'm pretty sure it's the wrong time of the month, thank goodness."

Disappointment covers his face, but then the corners of his mouth lifts. "More time to have you to myself. We'll just keep trying."

"Brick…" I start.

He leans over and kisses me and whispers, "Plus, you'll make a great mom." Yep, I'm pretty sure my ovaries just caught fire.

One of the women walks up to us, interrupting our talk. "Hey, Brick. Hi, Madison. I'm Avery. Do you want to go with me so we can find you some clothes to change into?"

I look over at Brick to see what he thinks. I've seen the sweet butts here and I don't think she's one of them, but I can't be sure. Brick nods his head at me.

"Sure, Avery. That would be great, since he won't let me leave." I thumb over at Brick.

He stares between the two of us and I'm surprised when a growl escapes his lips. Avery laughs and smiles up at him. "Easy, big guy. I'll bring her right back."

When we get to her room, she starts pulling out clothes for me. "So, uh, are you an old lady?" I ask her and hope I haven't offended her. I'm pretty sure that's what they're called.

She smiles while she sorts the clothes. "Well, Sniper says I am anyway."

I can't help but laugh. "I know what you mean. Brick's the same way."

We laugh and get to know each other. She gives me two changes of clothes and to heck with it, I even let her give me underwear. I'm definitely going to have to go shopping. I even had to use Brick's toothbrush today.

Once I change and put the extra clothes into Brick's room, I follow Avery back to the party.

7

BRICK

I watch as Madison walks out of the room. Several pairs of eyes follow them and I can't help the possessiveness rising in my belly.

I look around the party and one glance at the sweet butts in the corner dancing has me looking the opposite way. I have no interest in that anymore. I sit there, sipping the shot of tequila that Keeper gave me. We shoot the shit, and talk about the plan for the Fallen Kings.

Sniper joins us and I tell him I want to take Madison home with me, to my home.

"Well, if our intel is right, the Fallen Kings are on a run to Mexico. I had Smokey and some prospects check it out and their place is empty. You should be safe. It looks like we'll have a week before we have to worry about anything. Gives us time to get our shit together. No more surprises," he tells me.

I can hear it in his voice that he's even surprised the way everything went down last night.

"Everything okay, Brick?" he asks me.

I shake my head, like I've been thinking about something else. "Fuck no, it's not okay," I grunt back at him. "A woman had to save my ass. I'm losing my touch," I admit.

We watch as Avery and Madison walk back in. Madison has changed out of her waitress uniform and as she walks across the room, her eyes are on me.

"Fuck, I'm in trouble, Pres," I mutter to him.

"Yep." He laughs and slaps me on the back before going over to Avery.

I stay in my seat and wait on Madison to get to my side. "Let's get out of here."

"Where are we going?" she asks me.

"Home. I want to take you home," I tell her honestly. I've thought about it all day. Don't get me wrong, I love the club and my brothers, but I want my woman in my bed, in my home.

She looks up at me questioningly. "I thought we had to stay here, ya know, the Fallen Kings and all that."

I grab her hand and start walking to the door, nodding my head at the people that say bye to us. "That's club business, princess. I can't tell you about that. All you need to know is that you're safe and I would never put you in harm's way."

"So I can go home?" she asks me.

"Yes. To my, I mean, our home," I tell her before plopping the helmet on her head. I sit down on the seat and hold my hand out to her.

I'm ready for her to resist me, to tell me no, but instead she just shrugs her shoulders. "Okay, sounds good, Ben."

MADISON

Two Years Later

"Princess, you better be resting," I hear as the front door slams.

Ben was only gone for an hour. Since we're getting close to the due date, he rarely leaves me alone now.

I prop my swollen feet up on the chair across from me with my school book in my lap. It's taken a while, but I will be graduating next month. Even though I resisted it, Ben reasoned with me and finally convinced me to finish my schooling. He even promises to put me to work at one of the shops after I graduate, and well, after I have this baby that is dancing on my bladder.

He walks in and bends down to kiss me. "How you doing, princess?"

"Grrrr. You don't want to know," I tell him and try to adjust myself in the chair. I can't get comfortable these days.

"I know what you need," he tells me and turns around to the stove. I watch his ass move in the tight jeans and my mouth starts to water. *Damn hormones.*

The last two years have been a whirlwind. That day I gave in to his insistence that we were meant to be, and I gave in to what I really wanted, well, was the best decision I've ever made. Getting on the back of his bike started our relationship. We still joke about how I saved him… but really, he saved me too. I moved in with Ben the second night after knowing him and we haven't spent a night apart since. He's had obligations to the club, but he always makes sure to make it back to me before I lie down in bed.

My big ol' biker has proven to be a wonderful husband. We got married mere weeks after meeting. And he never asked me; nope, he told me we were. But of course, I didn't argue with him about it. I wanted it just as bad as he did.

He turns back toward me and gives me a mug with hot chocolate in it. He kisses me and then sits down in the chair across from me, picking up my legs and putting them in his lap.

Brick

I KNOW SHE'S MISERABLE. I can see it in her face. If there was anything I could do to help her, I would. I've talked to her doctor plenty of times until he's now told me not to call him until she's in labor.

Fuck, I don't know how I'll handle that.

She's reading her textbook and every now and then looking up at me. I'm rubbing her feet and thinking about her and all we've gone through.

The Fallen Kings eventually came back to town... and they didn't forget about what happened. They threatened us and Madison's life. Luckily, we already had a plan in action before they got back. We may or may not have had something to do with the raid that went down at their club. Sometimes it pays to have the police on your side.

Sometimes my chest gets tight just thinking of losing her and I can't focus, I can't work, I can't do anything. In those times, I always find my way back to her and hold her close.

"You're not drinking your cocoa," I comment.

She shakes her head side to side. "Nope, I wasn't really wanting cocoa."

I run my hand up and down her legs and I can see the desire in her eyes. "Oh yeah? What did you want?"

She slowly puts her feet on the ground. "My husband. In bed. With me."

I nod my head at her. "I think I can make that happen."

"I love you, Ben."

"I love you too, princess."

Keep Reading for Rancher's Story

RANCHER

1

RANCHER

I GRIP THE CRUTCHES IN MY HAND AND THROW THEM to the floor before falling to the couch. "Fuck!" I scream at the top of my lungs. I lean forward and rest my head in my hands.

I've dealt with a lot in my lifetime. The death of my parents, the death of my comrades in war, my wife leaving me while I was in the army. I've handled it all, and pretty well, I'll admit.

But this, this fucking injury is going to kill me. I can't do anything. I can't ride my hog, I can't ride my horse, I can't take care of my ranch, I'm a fuckin' liability with the club. I can't do nothin'.

A loud knock sounds on my front door and I don't even attempt to get up. I'm hoping that whoever it is, they take the hint and just leave.

But of course, I have no such luck.

"Rancher! Where are you, brother?" I hear

Sniper and the sound of multiple boots stomping across the floor.

"In here," I holler, leaning my head back on the couch. I'm preparing myself for what I know is about to happen. This isn't the first time that they've come and tried to get my ass off the couch.

They walk in, Sniper, Brick, and Keeper, members of the Exiled Guardians, the club that I'm a patched member and road captain of. Well, was. I can't be any kind of road captain if I can't get my ass on a bike. Instantly, I get pissed off because of the looks on their faces. That's the same look every brother in the club has given me… pity.

"What do you want?" I ask them.

I was in a bar fight a few weeks ago and tore ligaments in my leg. They say I should be okay, but I've had to take a few weeks to heal before starting physical therapy. I went to one session and quit. I told them I thought it was a waste of time, but honestly it was because I couldn't do half of what they asked me to do and it was frustrating as hell.

"We brought you something," Sniper offers.

"Well, unless it's the Fallen King that jumped me and put a knife into my leg, I don't want it."

Sniper shakes his head, and honestly I don't blame him. I know I shouldn't be talking to him like this. He's taken a lot of my shit, but I'm pretty sure my time is running out.

He smacks his hand to his leg and looks at me

fiercely. "Ranch, you know he was dealt with. We weren't going to let them get away with it."

I nod my head and lay it back again, closing my eyes.

"All right, boys, well, if that's it, you can leave now." I wait to hear the shuffling of feet, but don't hear any.

Then out of nowhere, I hear a soft feminine voice, "Yeah, boys, it's fine, you can leave now. I got this."

I open my eyes and my head jerks up, looking for the source of that voice and I'm not disappointed when my eyes land on the absolute prettiest filly I've seen in a long time. She's curvy, with long red hair in a ponytail and bright green eyes that are sparkling back at me from the other side of the room. She's covered in what looks like a nurse's uniform, but it does nothing to hide her curvy body.

I peek over her shoulder and Smoky follows in behind her, carrying a suitcase. "Miss Lane, I'm going to take this to the spare bedroom."

She never takes her eyes off me, but she thanks Smoky for carrying her bags.

I lean forward and rest my hands on my knees. I want to get up, but refuse to do so with so many people watching me. "Well, now, boys, this is more like it. Finally, you brought me something I will like."

Keeper steps in front of the goddess and blocks

my view. He walks toward me with his hands up. "Rancher, it's not like that. She's a physical therapist. She's going to stay here for a while and help you use that leg again."

"Fuck, no she ain't," I yell at him and then remember my manners. "Sorry, ma'am. No offense."

She looks surprised by my apology, but accepts it readily. "None taken."

"I'm not doing it, Keeper. Y'all can just take her back wherever you got her. I can figure this out on my own," I tell the lot of them fiercely. I hate being like this. I hate being weak.

The woman that will probably be starring in my dreams tonight walks toward me and sits on the edge of the coffee table right in front of me. Her knees are touching my legs and I swear I can feel my cock twitching at her closeness. I fight the urge to adjust myself. It's been too damn long since I've been buried in pussy, I tell myself. But honestly, I know I've never had pussy like hers. Her smell, a fresh lavender scent, hits my nose and I take a deep breath in until I realize what I'm doing and the fact that I'm still surrounded by bikers.

"Sniper, Keeper… you all can go. I got this from here," she tells them but still doesn't look away from me.

Keeper walks up behind her. "Rancher, are you

okay with this? I don't want you kicking her out and her having to walk back into town."

I stare at her a few seconds, but she doesn't seem affected by Keeper's train of thought.

I glance up at him. "Keeper, I think you know me better than that."

She smiles up at Keeper. "Thank you for your concern, but I'll be fine. No worries here."

I smile at her. She thinks she's won, but she hasn't. I'll let her stay, because fuck, I'd be dumb to kick her out. But I'm not going to let her "work" on me. No, I have other plans for her.

"You heard her, boys. She's good. See ya tomorrow."

Zoey

I WAIT until the other men walk out of the house before I say anything else to him. I use that time to try and get myself collected. When the bikers showed up at the clinic today, I couldn't help but be interested in what they had to say.

The way they talked about their "brother," well, they may be big, burly, tattooed men, but they also seem to be genuinely worried about him. They came prepared too. They handed me his folder and after reading the doctor's notes and seeing his file, I knew I could help him. I felt it to my core that this was something I needed to do.

So here I am, sitting on a strange man's coffee table in his house, watching him watch me.

I smile and hold my hand out to him. "I'm Zoey, by the way. Your friends told me to call you Rancher, not Michael."

He looks at my hand before reaching out and wrapping his around it. Mine looks so small in comparison.

He smiles at me with a nod, and I ignore the jolt I feel in my lower belly. "Zoey? That's a unique name."

I shrug my shoulders and pull my hand back from him. "Yep."

His hands go to my knees and slide up my thighs. I don't let him see my body tremble and I hope he doesn't notice the goosebumps on my arms. "So, Zoey, I have a bum leg, but I can think of a few things to keep us busy."

I put my hand on top of his to stop them and then I get up and put some distance between us. "I have plenty of plans for you, Rancher. But not tonight. We'll get started tomorrow morning."

He just shakes his head. "Nope, I'm not interested. The only thing I want from you is to tuck me in."

I cross my arms across my chest. I hope this isn't the real Rancher. I'm hoping this is some kind of defense mechanism, because honestly, this Rancher is an ass. A handsome ass, but still an ass. "With my help, you'll be walking without a limp in six to eight weeks. The damage is minimal."

Surprise garners his face. "No way."

I scrunch my nose at him. I wouldn't lie to him and I tell him that. "I looked at your file. With the right amount of therapy, you will definitely be walking again without the help of these." I gesture to the crutches I pick up off the floor and lean against the couch so he'll be able to reach them.

He still looks at me skeptically. I put my hand on my hip, a little offended. "Do I need to promise you? Swear on a Bible? Pinky promise? What?"

He struggles to his feet and stands up without the help of his crutches. Oh yeah, this will be a piece of cake.

"And I won't have a limp?"

I blow out a breath. I can hear the desperation in his voice. This is not a man that is used to being down. "Rancher, there are no guarantees. But I feel one hundred percent certain that I can help you. Will this leg bother you? Probably when it rains or if you are on it without rest for long periods of time. But you will be able to ride your bike, your horse, whatever you want to ride again."

He looks at me for a minute, like he's trying to see if I'm being completely honest with him. I don't look away, no matter how uncomfortable I am. This is too important. I want him to trust me. But I don't want him to see the attraction on my face either.

When he finally nods, he mutters, "Tomorrow then."

I turn quickly and start walking to the hallway, relieved to put some space between us.

"Second door on the left," he yells. "Right next to my room, honey. Just holler if you need me."

2

RANCHER

I COULDN'T SLEEP ALL NIGHT. I TOSSED AND TURNED thinking about Zoey in the room right next to mine. Am I excited to think that I might be able to walk without a limp? Absolutely. But what I can't get my mind off is Zoey.

I heard her moving around her room a few times, probably putting away her things. And that had me thinking about the fact that she's probably naked or in some nightgown right now, and my cock stayed hard all night.

I struggle through a shower and go to the kitchen at five am to start a pot of coffee. Looking out the window, I can already see a few of my brothers have arrived to help with the animals. My brothers have really stepped up. I would have lost the ranch without them.

I see Smoky pulling in on his hog, dust from the

dirt road flying behind him. I'm sure he was at his club last night until around three am. He owns the strip club in town. He has every excuse not to be here, but he still shows up every day.

Lost in thought, I startle when I hear "Good morning" from behind me.

Turning around, I see Zoey standing in the doorway watching me.

"Mornin'," I say and gaze down her body. She's wearing a pair of blue jeans and a V-neck shirt that is stretched across her large breasts. "How about breakfast?"

"Sure, I'll just have some fruit or some yogurt." She walks over to the refrigerator and pulls a little carton out.

I look between the carton and the fridge. "Where'd that come from?"

She starts opening drawers until she finds the silverware. "Oh, Keeper actually thought of it. He had me make a list of what I like to eat and he went to the store and brought it with us last night."

I turn my head side to side and crack my neck. It's a bad habit that I started in the army. It's what I do when I get uncomfortable about something. And right now, I'm uncomfortable. I don't like the fact that Keeper is looking out for her. Thinking back to how protective he was with last night, well, I don't know, makes me mad, to tell you the truth.

I gesture to the small carton in her hands.

"That's all you're going to eat? That's not enough to feed you."

As soon as the words come out of my mouth, I realize my mistake. Her eyes widen and shock hits her face. She clears her throat. "Yeah, I know for a big girl like me it's not much, I guess, but it's good enough. I'm going to set things up. After you eat, meet me in the living room and change into some shorts."

She stalks from the room and instantly I'm upset with myself, probably more than she is. Fuck, I'm not used to women and I wasn't saying anything about her weight. She looks perfect to me.

I put some bread in the toaster and open the fridge. Cracking a few eggs, I fry them up real quick and eat my breakfast. That's about the only thing I do quick these days. Trying to do anything else with these crutches makes me work twice as hard and I think about bringing her food as a peace offering, but I decide the best thing for me to do is not mention food to her today.

Zoey

I JUST FINISHED SETTING up the table in the living room. I have my tools set out.

I realize now that I've already made a fool of

myself. I'm usually not so sensitive about my weight. Honestly, I know what he said was not meant to hurt my feelings.

I can feel my heart beating in my chest, knowing that I'm going to have to apologize to him.

I'm reaching down to get more things out of my bag when I hear him walk in.

I stand up, all ready to apologize when my mouth falls open.

He's standing in the doorway wearing only a T-shirt and a pair of boxers.

"Sorry, Zoey. I don't have shorts. I'm a rancher and a biker. Neither one of those things really call for shorts."

Flustered, I look away. "It's fine. No problem." *I can handle this*, I tell myself. He's just another patient. It is wildly inappropriate for me to have these feelings toward a patient. *Hands off, Zoey*. But really, my hands are going to be on him. *You're a professional*, I keep chanting in my head.

"Climb up here." I pat the therapy bed.

He walks over toward me with the help of the crutches. He pulls himself up on the bed and flinches. I know men like Rancher. He hates for people to see him like this. I turn away and busy myself until he's settled.

Turning back to him, I inspect his leg. I look over his stab wound and it seems to be healing

118

perfectly. The damage he did was mostly from his fall.

I grab the heating pad and place it over the tight muscles, hoping to loosen them up before we get started.

He's lying back and his eyes are closed, so I watch him for a second before clearing my throat. "So about this morning, I'm sorry I overreacted."

He doesn't respond for a moment, making me wonder if he heard me or maybe I pissed him off. But then he opens his eyes. "I didn't mean anything by it. I think you are perfect the way you are."

Just that one sentence from him has me almost tearing up. I start to turn away, but he grabs my hand. "Hey, you okay?"

"Yeah, yeah, I'm fine. You just need to keep the heating pad on for a few more minutes and then we'll get started. I'll be right back."

I walk out of the room, leaving him on the bed. I rush back to my room and shut the door and lean against it.

I can't do this. I can't. I should have known when I read his file, and was drawn to it, to him, that there were red flags.

He's too much for me to resist. I can't lose my job. Hell, I'll lose my license.

I take a few deep breaths to calm myself and walk back to the living room. I walk up to him and avoid looking at his face. Removing the heating pad, I work in silence. Usually, I tell the patient what I'm doing step by step. Today, I don't do that. I don't say anything. Not until I'm massaging the tight muscles of his thigh that I notice the bulge in his shorts expanding so much that I'm sure his dick is about to come out of them.

I pull my hands back. "Oh!"

I look at Rancher and his eyes are filled with heat and desire, but also embarrassment. "Zoey, I know I've been an ass to you, but honestly, I didn't do this on purpose. It's just you, being this close with your hands on me, it just happened. I'm sorry. I tried counting back from a hundred, hell, I tried thinking of anything but your hands on me. Nothing worked."

I clear my throat again and look back at his penis and then to his face again. *Normal. It's normal*, I tell myself. I hold my hands up. "No need to apologize," I reassure him. "It's nothing to be embarrassed or ashamed of. It's a natural response. It happens."

He jerks up and leans on his elbows. "Other bastards get hard-ons when you work on them?"

Taken back, I answer him honestly. "Well, no, it's never happened with me, but I've heard it's happened before with other therapists." I go and grab a blanket off the couch and cover his lower body with it. As I'm arranging the cover, I stroke along his hard cock with the back of my hand and he moans.

"Shoot, I'm sorry. God, I'm so sorry." I cover my face with my hands. *Darn it, get yourself together, Zoey.*

3

RANCHER

THE REST OF THE SESSION IS UNEVENTFUL. AS SOON as we get through the embarrassing situation, I get up from the table and make my way back to my room. Before the door fully closes, I have dropped my crutches, my boxers are down around my ankles and my cock is in my hand. It only takes a few strokes before I'm moaning Zoey's name and spewing my cum on the bedroom floor.

Knock, Knock

"Rancher, you okay? I thought I heard the crutches fall. Do you need my help?" she calls through the door.

Fuck. I lean my head back against it and try to catch my breath. "No, I'm fine," I tell her, but really, I want to beg her to come in here so we can take care of each other.

There's no way I can continue this. She thinks

we are going to have another session later today. She's mistaken.

I get dressed, grab the crutches and walk past her on the way to the front door. "I'll be out at the barn," I tell her before slamming the door behind me.

Smoky and Keeper see me coming and meet me next to my horse, Dagger.

I pet him and God, what I wouldn't give to be out riding him.

Keeper hands me a piece of apple. "Your color already looks better and you're off the couch. Is it safe to say that we made the right decision bringing Zoey here?"

I feed the fruit to Dagger and shrug my shoulders. "She says she can help me walk without a limp. We'll see."

Smoky comes up behind us and looks toward the house. Even from here, we can see her standing in the big bay windows. "Well, if nothing else, she's a damn fine woman to look at. I might have to get injured after this just to get her hands on me."

My fists clench on to my crutches. "Fuck you, Smoky. That's not going to happen."

He eyes me speculatively. "Oh, is that how it is?"

"That's the way it is, fucker, so quit looking at her," I tell him and reach my crutch out to hit his legs.

He sidesteps it easily and starts laughing. "Don't worry, I'll wait until she realizes what a stubborn ass you are, then make my move."

"Har, har, you think you're funny."

We stand around and shoot the shit for awhile and I thank them for taking care of the animals. I watch as they drive off and then hang out at the barn for the rest of the day. I'll probably regret it later, and my leg will give me fits, but the more time I have away from her the better.

When it starts getting dark, I hear the crunch of gravel and know that she's finally come looking for me.

I've spent most of the day doing easy jobs to do the upkeep of the barn, but in fact, I just wanted to keep busy and stay far away from her. I know I've hit on her, but I'm sure today, I crossed some moral line. Yes, I want her. But I also don't want her to feel uncomfortable either.

"Rancher, where are you?"

I step out of the stall and look at the other end where she's standing in the doorway.

Zoey

HE'S AVOIDED me all day. Either to get out of the therapy or to get rid of me—which it is, I'm not sure. I walk over and look up at him. Thankfully, he's using his crutches but who knows how hard he's pushed himself today.

"Hey, I fixed dinner. I figure if you're not going to show up for therapy, I could at least earn my keep around here." I laugh, but a part of me is being serious. I caught up on patient notes and straightened up the living room and then spent the rest of the day reading romance novels.

"I'm not hungry," he grunts at me and right then his stomach growls.

Laughing, I touch his arm. "Your stomach is saying differently."

He freezes under my hand and I pull it back from him. "Okay, obviously you just don't like my company. I can have another therapist come out."

I look up at him and wait for a response, but he won't look at me. I give him plenty of time, but he says nothing.

I try to keep the hurt off my face, but I know it's there. I start to walk away to go pack my bags.

"Wait."

His gruff voice stops me, but I don't turn around.

He grunts and starts walking toward me, the frustration with his crutches apparent when he cusses as he fumbles with them.

"I don't want you to leave. Unless you think you should."

I turn to look at him with my forehead creased. "I don't understand. Should I think I should leave?"

He shrugs his shoulders.

"Look, obviously you're not comfortable with me being here. I think it would be easier on you if you had another therapist. I'm going to go pack my things."

"No!" His hand comes out and cups my shoulder, holding me still. When I turn around, he pulls it away. "I want you to stay. But I don't want you to be uncomfortable doing it."

I start to shake my head, but then it hits me. "You're talking about this morning?"

He nods. "Yeah, I know I've joked around with you, but I would never do anything, at least on purpose, to make you feel uncomfortable. I mean, I can't control my body's reaction to being near you, but I would never act on it or try to force myself on you or anything."

I can tell he's uncomfortable. *Has he worried about this all day?* "Can we talk about this inside at the table?" I ask. "The food is in the warmer, but I'm starving."

He looks at me skeptically, like he expects me to go off on him or something. Finally, he nods his head.

We walk side by side back to the house. I take it slow, not wanting him to feel rushed on my account.

When we walk in, the smell of pasta and garlic bread hits us.

"Is that spaghetti?" he asks me.

"Yep. Why don't you get cleaned up and it will be ready."

He's gone only a few minutes before he's back in fresh clothes and his wet hair is slicked back from his face.

We sit down and start eating. He moans between bites and it makes me wonder how long it's been since he's had a home cooked meal.

We eat in silence, and I keep taking peeks at him, watching him enjoy his meal.

"So, uh, I feel like I need to say it. You didn't make me feel uncomfortable this morning. I'm not worried about my safety or anything like that. I know you're a good guy," I start to tell him and then take a drink of water to stall a little.

His hand slides across the table and right before I think he's going to touch my hand, he wraps it around the edge of the table and squeezes it.

"I'm not a good guy, Zoey. Don't think that. You wouldn't think that if you knew what I've been thinking about all day."

"What have you been thinking?" I ask him and then cover my mouth with my hands. *Did I really just ask him that?* "Forget it, I don't need to know. It doesn't matter. This"—I point between the two of us—"can't happen. I'm here to get you walking. I can't get involved with patients."

He releases the edge of the table and slides his hand toward my arm. We both watch him move and I tremble at the thought he's going to touch me.

When his hand wraps around my forearm and his thumb strokes across my wrist, I fidget in my seat. His touch makes me want things I shouldn't.

"All I've thought about all day is your hands on me. All I've thought about, all fuckin' day, was putting my hands on you. I'm hard now, just thinking about it. If you stay here, Zoey, I'm not going to be able to stay away from you. I want you too damn much."

"I can't," I squeak. "I could lose my job." I jump up from the table and start piling the dishes in the sink. I start to wash them and when I look over my shoulder, Rancher is getting up and walking from the room. Man, I wish things were different.

4

ZOEY

I stay awake all night. When I think I'm about to fall asleep, I jolt awake. When I first went to bed, I had plans to quit the next morning and send another therapist. That is the legal and moral thing to do. The right thing.

The more I thought about it, the more shady it got in my head.

All I could think about is how I always do the right thing. I've never strayed from it; I've always done what was right and expected of me.

Well, now for the first time, I want something really bad. I want Rancher. He's a good man, and he's hurting. I want to be here for him and not just as his physical therapist.

When I ask myself, *Can you walk away from him tomorrow?* The answer is no. Absolutely not.

So I come up with a plan. And a prayer that I'm making the right decision.

I make a few phone calls the next morning and hide out in my room until everything is in place.

When I finally come out, I go to the kitchen and Rancher is sitting there at the table. He looks up at me and in that one look, I know I'm making the right decision.

"Can we talk?"

Rancher

I KNOW what she's going to say even before she says it. I nod and she sits down. I brace for what I know is coming. She's quitting on me. On us.

She nervously rubs her hands together. "Rancher, I made a few phone calls this morning. You have a new therapist showing up tomorrow."

There's no sense in arguing. She's obviously made up her mind.

"Uh, and if it's okay, well, God how do I even say this, I took two weeks vacation and I thought I could stay here… maybe help a little… as your friend." She looks away from me, but not before I see the insecurity in her eyes.

"Wait." I hold my hands up. "You're staying?"

She shrugs her shoulders. "Yes, but not as your therapist. Of course I will still help you while I'm here, but yes, I would like to stay. But I could only take off two weeks. And you won't be my patient."

I'm confused for a minute and then it hits me and I realize what this means.

I reach over to her and pull her hand toward me until she's out of her seat and on my lap.

She makes sure to avoid my bad leg as she turns sideways, smiling at me. She cups my face in her hands. "I may not have thought this through. You may not want me here for two weeks. Maybe you wanted one night. And honestly, that's fine, Rancher. I'll take whatever you are willing to give me, because the way I feel when you touch me, well, I just want to feel that again."

"Honey, you'll be lucky if I let you leave in two weeks." I kiss her then and it's just as sweet and primal as I thought it would be. Her lips touch mine and I get lost in it, not coming up for breath until I'm breathing raggedly.

"Go to the bedroom, my bedroom, honey. I'll be right there." I help her off my lap and watch as she stands over me.

"Let me help you, Rancher." She reaches for the crutches but I stop her.

"No!" I say, probably too harshly. I don't want her to see me struggling and I don't even know how

I'm going to pull off having sex. But I know that nothing will stop me from having her.

I soften my voice. 'I'm fine. I'll be right there."

She nods, and I watch her walk away.

I take a deep breath and struggle to get up. Once standing, I use my crutches to go to the bedroom.

She's watching me as I walk across the room to her. She wastes no time and

undoes my pants and pulls them, along with my underwear, down my hips and thighs.

"Sit down," she orders me.

I sit down on the bed and she takes the crutches from my hands. Without a word between us, she finishes pulling my pants off and my shirt up and her hands start caressing my shoulders and chest.

She looks at me in awe and pride fills me. "I wondered what you would look like—I mean, I imagined, but goodness, Rancher, nothing could have prepared me for this."

My hands go to her hips and I squeeze them. She has thick thighs and the image I've had in my head was of me bending her over and taking her from behind. But that can't happen, at least not today.

"I need to see you, too, honey," I tell her and start pulling at her clothes.

She makes fast work of taking them off and when she's standing before me with not a stitch of clothes on, I moan at her perfection. Her curvy body is everything I imagined it would be, but better.

"You're beautiful, Zoey." I stroke my hands across her chest, rolling her hard nipples between my thumb and forefinger. I pull her face up to look at me. "Honey, you'll have to be on top, but I promise to make it up to you later."

She smiles understandingly. "Rancher, I don't mind. I just want you."

I try to pull her up my body, but she stops me.

Shaking her head side to side, she tells me, "Scoot back."

I do as she says. She climbs up and with her hand on my chest, she pushes me backward until my back hits the bed and my head is on the pillow. She positions herself between my legs and when I look down at her, my swollen, hard cock is sticking up between us. She smiles at me as she lowers her head and kisses the tip.

My hips jerk at the contact. Her hair tickles my thigh and I move it out of her face so I can see her.

She sticks her tongue out and strokes it up and down my shaft. Her warm wet mouth swallows my cock and she starts sucking me in, moving her head up and down. "Come around here, honey," I say. "I want to taste you too."

She climbs over my legs and brings her lower body to where I can reach it with my hand. I touch her wet slit and stroke my fingers through her folds. Fuck, her cunt is warm and drenched. I slap her ass gently. "Climb up here, baby."

She pops off my cock and looks at me over her shoulder. "No, Rancher…"

I swat her ass again and then rub it gently.

"Michael, I want you to call me Michael. And don't tell me no on this, baby. You know you want my mouth on you," I urge her.

She presses her ass into my hand but doesn't do what I asked her to do.

"I'm not sitting on your face, Michael," she says and then puts her mouth back on my cock.

I lift her leg up, the one closest to my head and pull her over me, until her wet pussy is sitting on my face and I'm breathing her in.

I latch my lips to her swollen clit and she bucks against me.

"Argh!" she moans with my cock in her mouth.

I take my hands and spread her open, licking her until she's bucking against me. Her thighs tighten around me but I don't stop. I keep working her clit until her pussy heats up and she's flooding me with her hot juices.

"Michael, yes! Yes!" she hollers, thrusting against me.

Her strokes on my cock are deeper and I'm passing the back of her throat with every thrust.

"Zoey!" I say to her, but she keeps sucking me in.

"Zoey!" I try again. "Turn around, baby, I don't want to come until I'm buried deep inside you."

She moans and then her lips smack as she pulls off me. I help her move around until she's straddling my hips. Rising up on her knees, she lines me up at her center and slowly slides down my shaft. Her tight pussy clenches on to me and I'm fighting the urge to come and I haven't even pumped once.

"Hold still, baby." I grip her hips. "Just for a minute."

I unclench my eyes and look up at her. She's a goddess sitting astride me, her perfect round breasts thrust out, her curvy stomach and thighs, damn, I can't take it.

"Ride me, Zoey. Bounce on my cock," I urge her, with my hands on her hips helping her lift up and down.

She angles her hips to the left, then to the right, springing up and down. I squeeze her tightly, and for a minute, I wish I could roll her over and thrust deep inside of her like I want to. She leans backward with her hands on the bed and rides me, with my cock hitting her G-spot.

"Yes, Michael, don't stop. I'm coming. I'm coming."

I come then. I shoot my hot seed deep inside of her and grunt her name as I give her all I've got.

When we both come down, her pussy is still pulsating around me with tiny vibrations.

Hours later, when we are both so exhausted from another round, I hold her to me while she snores softly against my chest. Yeah, two weeks is not going to be enough.

5

RANCHER

I WAKE UP THE NEXT MORNING AND FEEL THE BED next to me. It's empty. I raise up and look around the room, but Zoey is gone.

I grab my crutches that are leaning against the nightstand and gingerly get out of bed.

After taking a quick shower, I walk into the kitchen and find her standing by the big window, looking out on the ranch. The men are pulling out of the driveway and I realize that I must have slept really late this morning.

Walking up behind her, I wrap my arms around her and pull her to me. She turns her head to the side to look up at me, and I kiss her lips. "Mornin', honey."

"Morning. I thought I was going to have to come and wake you up. Your new physical therapist will be here any minute."

She kisses me once more and then goes to the oven and pulls out a plate of bacon and eggs. Setting them on the table, she tells me, "if you want breakfast, you better eat. You don't have much time."

As I sit down, she leans down and kisses my head, then tells me she's going to get the living room ready.

I eat quickly, not wanting to be away from her. I walk into the living room, slide onto the table and then lean the crutches against the couch.

"Breakfast was good."

She smiles at me. "Thanks!"

She's laying out instruments, and I can't resist teasing her. "So, is today's therapist as hot as you?"

She laughs. "Oh, hot. Definitely hot."

The doorbell rings and she smirks at me before she goes to open it. Something tells me there's something up.

When she walks back in, I figure out why.

"Bruce, this is Rancher. Rancher, Bruce. He is your new therapist."

The man beside her is huge, probably the size of Brick. He's smiling at me and cracking his knuckles. Something tells me I should be scared.

"Well, I'm going to go shower," she tells me before touching Bruce on the shoulder, "Be good to him, Bruce."

"Uh, uh, Zoey. Get back over here," I tell her.

Later, I'm going to talk to her about touching other men, no matter how innocent it is. For now, I'm going to make sure I get that kiss before she leaves.

She walks slowly over to the table with a worried expression. "You okay?" She must see my frustration and I try to relax the strained look on my face.

"Yes, I'm fine. But I want a kiss before you leave," I tell her, wanting to make sure that Bruce knows what's up.

"Rancher!" she gasps.

I simply shrug my shoulders and pucker up.

She bends over and kisses me briefly before turning to go out of the room. I don't even see it, but I know her face is blood red.

"So that's how it is?" Bruce asks her with an approving smile on his face.

She nods her head, looks at me over her shoulder and then back at Bruce. "Yep, that's how it is."

Zoey

I GO to the bathroom and strip off my clothes. I put off showering because I like having Rancher's smell on me. My thoughts go back to the night before. He is an unselfish lover and my body hurts in muscles I didn't even know I had. He made me feel things last night I've never felt before. In the middle of the night, we talked about birth control, which I'm on. And we had the talk about being clean. It was a little irresponsible of us to wait until after the fact, but it all worked out. I thought I could do this. I thought I would have some fun and then be able to walk away. And I may not have a choice. But it may hurt a little.

From what I know of bikers, which isn't much, I thought for sure we would be one and done. I mean I've heard of the 'sweet butts' and the 'twinkies.' But he's not acting like he wants me gone this morning. I'm determined not to get my hopes up. I took the two weeks off because well, I wanted him and knew I couldn't have him if he was my patient. But I also took the time off because I know I'm the best. If I can help him and work with him these next two weeks, he will have a good start to healing.

I don't know why it's so important to me, but it is. I want him better. I don't want him to feel like less than a man just because he's injured. I mean, for goodness sakes, he's a veteran, a rancher, a biker… he's made of tough stuff.

After my shower, I lie down on the bed to read a little and before I know it, I'm being woken up by a warm body wrapped around me and a hard cock poking my hip.

Moaning, I circle in his arms and look at him. "I must have fallen asleep. Someone kept me up all night. How was your session?"

He brushes the hair off my cheek and tucks it behind my ear. "It was good. Fine. But I think I like you touching me better."

I laugh and snuggle into his chest.

He kisses the top of my head. "From now on, you sleep in my bed. I didn't like finding you in here."

We stare into each other's eyes and I feel like he's telling me something but I'm too afraid to ask what that is.

I simply nod my head and lay it down on his chest.

We spend the next few hours like this. Talking and laughing, thoughts of his injury far from thought. We're almost like a normal couple. Almost.

6

ZOEY

TWO WEEKS LATER

"What do you mean you want to go out tonight?" Rancher asks me.

I roll my eyes. *Really?* I think to myself. I've been here two weeks and we haven't gone anywhere. I mean the man doesn't even leave the house to go to the store; he has it delivered.

"We haven't left the house in two weeks. I go back to work tomorrow and I want to blow off some steam," I explain to him.

"Oh, honey, I got some steam you can blow off." He pulls me to him and smacks his hand across my ass.

I pull away from him and move out of his reach. "Nuh-uh, no way, you are not getting out of this. You are taking me out tonight."

His face is settled into a frown when he realizes that he's not going to be able to get out of this one.

He snaps his fingers. "I got it. How about I invite the girls over? You've gotten close with Avery and Madison and I can hang with Sniper and Brick."

"They are going to the clubhouse. There's a party tonight and I want to go," I tell him.

I watch his face and I can see the worry on it. He's come so far these last two weeks. He still uses the crutches but he has been able to put some weight on his leg. In a few more weeks, I doubt you'll even be able to tell he had an injury.

No, what I'm worried about is his frame of mind. He doesn't hang out with his brothers, even though they've asked him to many times. He hasn't been to the clubhouse in I don't know how long. He did finally start working his ranch and doing the things he's able to do. I've actually enjoyed working beside him, even though he gets upset with me when I try to pick up bales of hay or help him clean stalls.

"Fine. I was hoping we would be able to hang out tonight, but if you don't want to go, Smoky said he would come get me."

I turn around to walk off but he drops his crutches and then grabs me around the waist. "Fuck that, woman. You're not going anywhere with Smoky and you sure as hell are not getting on the back of anyone else's bike."

I back my ass into his stiff cock and turn my

upper body to look at him. Smiling, I ask him, "Okay, so you'll take me?"

He runs his hand up and down my back.

I'm wearing a short skirt, cowboy boots and a black blouse. I nixed the underwear, because well, he's ruined so many of them that I was waiting until we were about to leave before I put them on. No joke, the man has torn almost every pair.

"Fine, but you stay with me," he tells me gruffly.

I crease my forehead. "What else would I do?"

He shrugs his shoulders. "I hate to think of all those swinging dicks looking at you. I don't want to fight one of my brothers my first night back at the clubhouse."

I rub my ass against his front, and he reaches down under my skirt. When he touches bare skin I jerk at the electric charge his hand sends through me. "No underwear? You're not going to the club without any underwear on."

I roll my eyes. "I know that, but I am also down to one pair because someone keeps ripping mine. I'll put some on before we go."

His fingers explore my mound and stroke through my slit. He lifts my skirt up over my ass and caresses each cheek. He pushes me toward the edge of the couch to bend over, but I stop him.

"Here, sit on the edge." I know he wants to take me from behind but his balance isn't the best yet. I want to give him what he wants, though.

He sits down on the edge of the couch and I back up to him. I'm already soaked. Just being this close to him does that to me.

He grips my hips and I impale myself on him.

"I love having you inside me," I tell him as I move up and down.

His hands are squeezing my hips, helping me move on his hard shaft.

It doesn't take long before I'm coming all over his cock and milking him until every drop of his cum is inside me.

Rancher

I KNEW this was a bad fucking idea. I'm surrounded by my brothers, and honestly, I've missed this part. They've stood by me through so much and I wouldn't have made it without them. Plus, they are the ones that brought Zoey into my life. I owe them big just for that.

No, what's bothering me is watching Zoey on the other side of the room, dancing with Madison and Avery. Well, honestly, it pisses me off. Everyone here knows that Avery and Madison have been claimed by Sniper and Brick. No one will mess with them. Hell, they even have cuts on with a patch that says 'property of.' But Zoey is like a beacon of light that any man with a dick is going to hit on. I haven't claimed her, not properly, and I should have done that before I brought her here.

I've been on the edge of my seat all night, my hands fisted, ready to fight anyone that even talks to her.

"You fucking love her, don't you?" Smoky asks me and nods toward the dance floor.

I shrug my shoulders. Not because I don't know the answer, because I do. But what I think is that I should probably tell her first.

"Fuck that, all you pussies settling down. No woman is going to chain me down," he says and takes a shot of whiskey.

I could argue with him. I could tell him that two weeks ago I would have said the same thing. But instead, I just nod at him and keep watching Zoey.

One of the prospects is eyeing her and before he can get too close, I grab my crutches and start walking her way. I cut him off and lean down right in his face. "Don't even think about it, motherfucker."

He looks shocked, but he doesn't say anything. He just turns around and goes the other direction.

"Dance with me, Rancher," she asks as she comes up beside me.

I hold my crutches out to tell her no, but when I look at the happiness on her face, I can't turn her down. Her cheeks are rosy and I can tell she's having a good time. I'm not going to ruin it.

I lean my crutches against the wall and then circle my hands around her waist. We sway slowly to the sound of the music. Her eyes are on mine and there are so many things I want to say to her, but not now, not here.

Not with the sweet butts making out with members over in the corner, and not with all the drunks making noise and having a good time. I'm going to tell her when we get home… our home.

I close my eyes and lean my head against hers. I could do this all night.

I hear laughter and don't think anything of it until someone runs past us, knocking into me. I lose my balance and my leg gives out, causing me to go down. Which would be okay, but Zoey grabs me and I end up taking her down with me. We both land against the wall, but Zoey gets the brunt of it, hitting her face.

But she's not worried about herself or the knot already forming on her forehead. Nope, she's worried about me.

"Rancher, oh my God, are you okay?" She tries to help me up but I stop her, unable to take my eyes off the knot over her eye.

Smoky lifts me by the arms to bring me up and hands me my crutches.

"Zoey, your head. You're hurt," I tell her, moving in close, but not too close.

"What?" she asks. "I'm fine. Are you okay?"

The longer I stare at her, the madder I get. What kind of man am I? Hell, I can't protect her from anyone else if I can't even protect her from me. "I'm leaving. Are you ready?"

I start walking toward the front door with her by my side. The room is silent and I know my brothers will understand me leaving. I had thought Zoey would argue with me and want to stay, but she didn't. She is following me quietly out the door.

7

ZOEY

I DON'T EVEN KNOW WHAT'S HAPPENED. ONE MINUTE we're dancing and the next we're both lying against the wall. I'm so glad he didn't reinjure his leg, but from the looks of it, his pride is broken.

He doesn't talk to me the whole ride to his house. I start to speak a few times, but then change my mind. Maybe it will be better if I can look at him when I'm talking to him.

We pull up to his ranch and walk inside the house.

When I walk by the mirror in his entryway, I see my reflection and grimace at the bruise on my head. I don't stop to inspect it because I have a feeling that is one of the reasons he's so upset.

I sit on the edge of the couch, now a little nervous because he still hasn't said anything and it's driving me crazy.

"Say something, Michael."

He takes a deep breath and runs his hands through his hair. He sits down on the coffee table in front of me and pulls my chin so I'm looking up at him.

He winces when he looks at me.

"It doesn't even hurt," I tell him sincerely.

Pain is etched all over his face. "I did that to you."

I shake my head at his nonsense. "You didn't do this to me. The jerk that bumped into us did this."

He shakes his head. "Don't you see? I can't even protect you. What kind of man am I?"

"You're the best man…" I start to tell him.

He struggles to stand up and I instantly start to worry that he may have reinjured his leg, but he walks easily over to the crutches.

He's looking away from me. His voice is husky and filled with emotion. "It's probably best you leave in the morning, Zoey." He walks slowly out of the room and I sit there astounded at the turn of events.

I thought we were doing well. I know I was. I hate that the stupid jerk at the club knocked into us. But falling like that could have happened to anyone.

I sit there for the longest time, debating what to do.

I could leave and drive home tonight, but that doesn't feel right.

I don't want to leave period. In my heart, I've been hoping that we would continue our relationship past the two weeks.

I stand up and start pacing the living room floor. So many things are going through my head. But finally it hits me. I can't just leave. I can't walk away from him. I love him and I'm pretty sure he feels something for me too.

With determination, I stride from the room toward his bedroom. I open the door quietly, thinking that he may already be in bed.

But the sight before me about floors me.

He's sitting on the edge of the bed with his head in his hands. I stand there staring at the corded muscles of his back under his T-shirt, his broad shoulders and thick forearms. He's so handsome.

I start pulling off my clothes and slide under the covers next to him, rolling over so I'm facing his back.

"What are you doing, Zoey?"

"Well, one thing I'm not doing is leaving you," I tell him.

He shakes his head. "You're better off without me."

I raise up on my elbow. "You really think so? Because I think that if I left here, I'd be leaving part of my heart behind."

I can feel my heart racing in my chest. I know I could be reading this wrong and he could send me packing, but I have to at least try. For both our sakes.

He lifts his head up, still not looking at me. "But I hurt you…"

I interrupt him. "No, you didn't. I love you. How can I leave you knowing that?"

He turns then and looks at me. "You love me?"

I shake my head at him. "Yes, I fucking love you."

He starts to say something, but then stops. He stares back at me and I can see his mind racing. "Zoey, I love you too. But you deserve a better man than me."

Frustrated, I tell him heatedly, "There's not a better man than you, you stubborn ass. Look, I'm naked under here. I love you. You love me. We don't know what tomorrow brings. Hell, you might wake up and never want to see me again. But what I do know is that we have to try. If you love me like you say you do, then you need to forget everything else and just love me, Rancher. That's it, just love me. The rest will work itself out."

He pulls the covers back and lies down next to me. He slides against me and covers my hip with his hand. "I love you too much, Zoey. I can't give you up. Fuck, I know you deserve better, but I'm going to spend the rest of my life being the man that you need me to be."

I kiss his lips softly. "You're already all I need."

He pulls me across him and I lay my head on his chest. "You too, baby. You're all I'll ever want and all I'll ever need. Forever."

EPILOGUE

ZOEY

Three Years Later

THIS IS MY LIFE, AND IT'S BEYOND ALL MY DREAMS. We're cruising down a highway, and I'm on the back of Rancher's bike. I'm gripping him with my arms and my thighs. My life has changed so much in such a short time, but there's nothing I would change about it.

That night that Rancher told me he loved me, well, I woke up the next morning and he was working out.

He worked harder those next few weeks than I've ever seen anyone work in my life. One day, when Smoky was at the ranch, he commented that he could tell how hard Rancher was working. Rancher only commented, "I have to so I can marry my woman and take her on a honeymoon."

Eight weeks later and he was walking just fine, no limp. Every now and then it hurts him. It's usually when he rides his horse, but there's no way he's ever going to give that up. Plus I wouldn't want him to. He's a sight to see in a cowboy hat.

Twelve weeks after we met, we got married at the ranch. Everyone pitched in and it was perfect. Of course, it helped that I had my groom, the love of my life, waiting for me at the end of the aisle.

One year after that, we had our son. He's now almost a year old and Sniper and Avery are babysitting him. He is just like his daddy. Stubborn as all get out.

I am still working but I have taken my case load down to only two days a week. I like being home with MJ – Michael Junior. I'll probably pick up more hours when he gets older.

Rancher slows the bike down and pulls down a dirt path. Once he's parked, I hop off the side of the bike. Pulling my helmet off, I ask him, "What are we doing here?"

He puts the stand up on the bike and gets off. "Well, I can't remember the last time I've had my wife to myself, so I'm bringing you out to the middle of nowhere, so that no one can find us. There's no cell reception, I have a basket of food, a blanket… I figure we can, you know, hang out."

I tilt my head to the side and try not to laugh in his face. "You brought me out here to hang out?"

He shrugs, but I can see the glint in his eye. "Sure."

I smack his chest. "You brought me out here for sex, Rancher!" I laugh.

Sheepishly, he admits it. "Well, I've missed you. Things have been hectic and I just wanted us to reconnect, that's all. You know, without any inter-ruptions. I mean, come on, this parenting thing is tough."

I laugh, because he's right. I don't think MJ slept any of his first year. Or at least it feels like it. And with both of us working, and taking care of the ranch, well, it's a lot.

"Oh, I'm not complaining. I'm actually glad you thought of it. I could use some time with my handsome husband."

He lays the blanket down and holds his hand out for me to sit down.

Once I'm sitting next to him, I lean over and kiss his cheek before whispering to him, "Plus I'm not wearing any underwear."

"Fuck yeah," he moans and then he takes his sweet-ass time loving every inch of my body.

Keep Reading for Smoky's Story

SMOKY

1

SMOKY

Kristy, the woman grinding on my lap, is a dancer here at Teasers Topless bar, and yes, she's topless. In the past, I would takc her up on what she's offering. But these last few months, well, I just haven't been interested.

My hand is on her hip, while her hard, pebbled nipples are pressed against my chest. She's worked up and I know I don't even have to touch her for her to come pressed against my leg. She wanted me to take her upstairs to my apartment, but I refused. First of all, I never take a woman up there and second of all, I'm not interested. I lean over the invoice I'm reading, not even wanting to think about why I'm not interested. Why, normally, my cock would be hard begging to get out of my pants but right now, I'm flaccid as a wet noodle. I shake my head, thinking, *Fuck what's wrong with me?*

Knock. Knock.

My assistant manager, Teddy, knocks on the door and pushes it open. Kristy doesn't stop; she doesn't care that she's grinding on me with an audience.

I look up and Teddy rolls his eyes at Kristy before telling me, "The woman I hired yesterday is here to fill out paperwork. You want me to take care of it?"

I look behind Teddy, but can't see the woman behind him. I've always liked talking to the new hires, wanting to make sure they're a good fit. I mean, fuck, it ain't like this is rocket science, but I've learned you get one bad apple and it screws up the whole bunch.

"No, I got it," I tell Teddy. "Kristy, isn't it time for your shift?"

I deal with her pouting and she reluctantly gets off my lap with her bikini bottoms pushed into the crease of her twat. She doesn't even try to fix herself before getting up and glaring at Teddy as she stomps out the door.

Teddy steps to the side and pulls a woman into the room. Her eyes are wide as saucers as she watches Kristy walk out. Teddy gestures to me while speaking to her. "This is Smoky. He's one of the owners of the club. He'll help you with the paperwork and then I'll help you get started."

She blinks quickly and nods her head at him before turning to look at me.

I stare up at her and instantly think that she's the most beautiful woman I've ever seen. She's curvy, with long brown hair and big brown eyes. She has an innocence about her and my cock begins to twitch in my pants. I can't stop myself; I look down at my crotch and wonder if I'm imagining it, but the bulge gets bigger right before my very eyes.

I look back up at her and when she raises her eyes to meet mine, she gasps. I'm sure she can feel the heat coming off of me. I can't take my eyes off of her and a blush creeps across her cheeks.

Teddy leans across the desk and whispers, "Take it easy on this one."

I clench my fist at his words. Does he like her? Is he staking his claim on her? One look at her and I can see why. I nod and gesture for him to leave. I mean, after all, I am the owner.

I stand up to my full height and realize that I'm probably a foot taller than her. She is tiny compared to me. "So, what's your name?"

"Harper," she whispers, but doesn't raise her eyes.

"So, Harper?" I say, trying to get her attention.

She doesn't answer me, and she doesn't look up at me. She's busy staring at my leg. I look down at myself and see the dark, wet spot on my jeans where Kristy was just sitting. I take a deep breath as shame fills me. It's a feeling I'm not used to and it almost guts me.

I walk over to a closet and pull out an extra pair of pants. I start undoing my jeans when her eyes get even bigger and I can tell I'm scaring her.

I hold the pants in my hand. "Honey, I'm going to change my pants. You can watch if you want to, but if not, you may want to turn around."

I pull my jeans down my legs and she whips around to face the wall. I undress quickly and pull my clean jeans on, taking special care to not zip my hard cock up in the fastener.

When I'm done, I walk over to her and touch her on the shoulder. She jerks around and her long hair wisps across my face, the scent of cherries hitting my nose. I barely contain my groan. "I'm sorry for what you walked in on. It won't happen again."

Apologies are not my thing, and I don't know why it matters, but I don't want her to think badly of me. I blow out a breath, knowing that we are off to a rocky start.

She takes a step back from me and holds her hands up. "It's your club. None of my business. I just need a job."

I look down her body and back up again. If she thinks she's going to dance here, she's got another think coming. There's no way I'm going to let that happen.

"You're not dancing," I tell her.

She rolls her eyes at me. "I know that. I'm sure I would make more money waiting tables than dancing."

I look at her questioningly. Is she crazy? She would make a killing here dancing, I have no doubt. But I don't tell her that.

My shaft twitches in my pants and before she notices and takes off running out the door, I walk back to my chair and sit down.

"Have a seat."

She walks over and sits down also, staring at her hands in her lap.

I clasp my hands together and lay them on the desk in front of me. "Harper." I say her name, liking the sound of it. "So why do you want this job?"

She shrugs her shoulders. "Because I need the money?"

"Why?" I insist.

She shrugs her shoulders again, but this time doesn't say a word. I then ask her the question I need to know the answer to, the one that is burning a hole in my chest the longer I keep it inside. "Do you have a boyfriend? A husband? Or a dad that will have a problem with you working here?"

She doesn't want to answer. I can see it in her eyes. "Is it legal to ask me that?"

Probably not, I think to myself, but that still doesn't stop me. "You already have the job, but I need to know if you are going to be bringing problems here."

I stare at her until she's squirming in her seat. "Nothing is going to interfere with my job."

I lean forward. "Do. You. Have. A. Boyfriend?"

2

HARPER

I STARE BACK AT HIM. TALK ABOUT FIRST impressions, nothing like walking in on your boss while a woman is gyrating on his lap. Of course, I could barely see around Teddy, but I did see the woman with her naked breasts swaying back and forth as she moved. Once Teddy moved, and I was able to see the man behind the desk, it made sense. I can sort of see why a woman would dry hump his leg. He's big, covered in tattoos, and his voice is deep and scratchy. You would think he smokes cigarettes, but when he was close to me, I didn't smell it and I don't see an ashtray lying around.

He has short brown hair and gray eyes… and when he stares at me like he's doing now, I have to turn away. There's just something molten about him.

When he apologized to me for what I saw when

I walked in and then told me it wouldn't happen again, well, it surprised me and honestly, confused me a little. Obviously, there's something going on with him and that Kristy – why apologize?

Lost in thought, I realize I made a mistake when he reaches across the desk and pushes the hair out of my face. "Harper. Answer me."

Embarrassed to be caught staring at him and hoping that he can't read my thoughts, I almost shout at him, "No. No boyfriend. No husband. And as of two weeks ago, no dad."

He leans back then, and I swear I see a smug look on his face before it disappears, and then all I see is pity. "I'm sorry about your dad."

I simply shrug. I want to scream at him that his sorry is worthless, it's not going to bring him back, but I don't. It's not his fault that my mom died five years ago. It's not his fault that my dad finally drank himself to death mourning her. And it's not his fault that I'm about to lose the only home I've ever known. Nope, I need to get myself together, because I wasn't lying when I said I needed this job.

He grabs some papers out of the filing cabinet by his desk and while he's looking for them I can't help but appreciate his ass in his tight, worn blue jeans. He turns back to me and I flick my eyes back up to his face quickly. Damn it, caught! I can tell by the arrogant look on his face that he caught me staring. Oh well, I can control myself, and honestly,

SMOKY

I don't want a man that obviously has a woman already.

He lays the papers down in front of me and hands me a pen. I grab it, making sure that my fingers don't touch his.

He stands next to me for a few seconds and my hand trembles as I start to write. He shouldn't have this effect on me. I don't need a man like this, no matter how attractive he is.

"Can I have your driver's license and social security card?"

I reach for my purse and dig out my IDs, then lay them on the desk. He picks them up and walks with them to the copier. I watch him as he looks at them for a long time before finally making the copy.

When he turns back to me, I start writing again. "Twenty-one, huh?"

I glance up at him. "Yep."

He just nods his head and so I finish filling out the paper and sign my name, handing them back to him.

He holds my IDs out to me and this time, my fingers graze his. I can feel the heat coming off of him, and I almost bury my face in my purse acting like I'm having a tough time finding my wallet. But in truth, I need this break from him to compose myself.

I stand up. "I'm going to go find Teddy. He's training me, right?"

167

He immediately starts shaking his head side to side. "No, I'm going to train you, but I'm about to leave. So you'll start tomorrow."

I instantly start to freak out. I don't know how much in tips I will be making, but honestly, I was hoping to make something. My refrigerator is bare and I have to pay the electric by Friday.

"But I really need… well, I was hoping to start today." Normally, I would be embarrassed, but not now, not today. I need the money. I'm not too proud to admit it.

He stares back at me like he's trying to read my thoughts. I don't blink, and I stare right back. This is important to me.

"You'll get a night's pay and start tomorrow," he explains.

I cross my arms across my chest. "I don't need a handout. I want to work. Can I please start tonight?"

He looks like he's about to argue but stops himself. "Fine, but I want you with Teddy the whole night. No leaving his side. Anyone gives you a problem, you come talk to me about it. If I'm not here, you call me. Give me your phone."

I look at him incredulously. "What?"

His hand is in front of me with his palm up. "Give me your phone. I'm going to put my number in it."

I pull the band off my wrist and wrap it around

my hair, putting it in a ponytail. "I don't have a phone."

He picks the papers up that I just filled out and points at it. "So what's this number you put on here?"

"My home phone," I tell him, and then figure I should be honest about it. "But it's disconnected."

"Fuck," he grunts.

I take a step back from him. "I'll be here. You don't have to worry about me not showing up and you trying to get a hold of me or anything."

He takes a step toward me. "I'm not worried about that." He looks pissed for a minute before he finally unclenches his jaw. "Fine, I'll have Teddy keep an eye on you."

He opens the door and I slide by him to get out of the office. I don't wait for instructions. I see Teddy at the bar and start walking toward him.

Smoky pulls Teddy aside and I can tell they're talking about me, but I turn my back to them and try to act like I'm memorizing all the liquor bottles they have on hand.

I turn around when I feel a peck on my shoulder. "I'm sorry I have to leave. Club business," Smoky tells me. "I'll be back before your shift is over."

I just nod, not really understanding why he's explaining himself to me. He finally leaves, but does it reluctantly.

The rest of the night flies by. Teddy trains me quickly and it isn't long before I'm working the floor, delivering drinks. The dancers, for the most part, seem to be nice. All of them except Kristy, the one that I assume is Smoky's girlfriend. No, she has a bitchy remark every time I turn around. But I just ignore her. There's no sense antagonizing her and getting myself fired.

I keep checking the door, thinking Smoky will be back any minute, but he never does show up. I can almost kick myself. I know he's bad news. I just met him a few hours ago and I shouldn't care where he's at. I've found out that he's part of the Exiled Guardians, and my father has always warned me to stay away from them. I finish cleaning up and head out the door, putting my tips into my pocket. If the rest of this week goes as well as tonight, then I will definitely be able to pay the light bill, get food and even pay the water. Yes, things are looking up.

3

SMOKY

I WALK INTO THE BAR THE NEXT NIGHT AND FOR THE first time since I left her yesterday, a calm fills me. I told her that I would be back last night, and I fucking lied to her. Not that I had a choice. I had club business to take care of and it's not like I can put that shit off.

I sent one of the prospects to watch her for the night and when I found out she didn't have a car and was walking home, I about fucking lost it. I should have been there to take her home. But instead, I had to have the fucking prospect follow her to make sure she was safe.

I watch her carry a tray toward a table of men and watch as they all eye her. She has on one of the T-shirts with the bar logo on it and a short jean skirt that's frayed at the bottom. I follow the line of her thick thighs down her legs into her short boots.

Adjusting my hardening cock, I can't take my eyes off her. When one of the men talks to her and she laughs at whatever he says, I get pissed, wanting that laugh, that smile for me and only me.

I don't know what it is about this girl, but I haven't stopped thinking about her. I can't. She's got a tight hold on my testicles it seems and I don't know if I like it. I'm used to having women fall at my feet and the look she gave me when I walked in, like she couldn't give a flying fuck I was here or not, well, it goes all through me. I want her eyes on me and only me.

I watch her as she walks to another table and picks up some empty bottles and there's more talking, then she smiles at them before walking off. I kid you not, the whole table of guys watches her walk away. I know it's going to be a problem because our best dancer, KiKi, is shaking her stuff on the dance floor and instead of looking at her, these guys all have their eyes on Harper.

She walks up to the bar and places an order for some beers.

I walk up beside her and stand right next to her. She doesn't even acknowledge me. "This isn't working out, Harper."

She puts her hand on her hip. "Look, I can't help it your girlfriend doesn't like me. I've stayed out of her way and will continue to listen to her shit, but I need this job."

I sputter, "Girlfriend? I don't have a girlfriend."

She eyes me with a smirk and rolls her eyes. "Okay, fuck buddy, lady of the night, booty call, whatever you want to call her."

I crowd her then, because I swear I can feel the jealously coming off of her in waves. "I don't have one of those either. And especially not now. I haven't been interested in a while, at least not until yesterday."

She rolls her eyes at me and starts to say something and then stops.

I put my hand on hers on the bar. "No, tell me. What were you going to say?"

"You mean Kristy dry humping your leg yesterday? Well, if she's not your girlfriend, you may want to tell her that." She gestures behind me and I look across the room. Sure enough, Kristy is staring daggers at us and when I turn and glare at her, she looks away and starts dancing toward a table of men.

"Is she giving you problems?" I ask Harper.

"No. Nothing I can't handle. Why are you firing me?" she asks me and pulls her hand out from under mine.

"I'm not firing you," I tell her.

She puts the beers on her tray that Teddy set down in front of us. "Good." She turns away and I watch her walk to the group of men.

She drops off the beers, checks on a few other tables and comes back to the bar.

"Teddy, pull one of the dancers to help you. I need Harper."

Teddy looks like he's about to challenge me, but he must second-guess himself, because he simply nods and turns away.

Harper holds her hands up in front of her. "No, no way, I'm not going anywhere with you."

"Do you want a job?" I ask her, knowing that she needs this.

"Yes. But I think you've made a mistake. I'm not that kind of girl and I don't plan to be... no matter how hot you are."

She slaps her hand over her mouth, realizing that she said it out loud. *Oh, baby girl, you have no idea. You just sealed your fate.*

I grab her purse from under the counter. "I know you're not that kind of girl. That's why you're not waiting tables. I can't have you out there with all these men and be able to protect you. I want you working behind the bar."

Her eyes widen in shock. "Protect me? You don't need to protect me. And everyone has been so nice to me, there won't be a problem. Plus, I don't know the first thing about bartending."

I put my arm around her waist and start shuffling her to the door. "I figured as much. That's why I'm taking you to the club, to get you trained."

She stops walking and whirls around. "Club? We're at the club!"

"No, my club. We're going there, where Keeper can train you and I don't have to worry about you getting hit on. One glance from me, and none of my brothers will even think about touching you."

She holds her hands up and puts them on my chest to stop my advance. The heat from her hands does something to me. I look down at her long fingers as they curl into my chest. I cover one hand with mine and hold it.

Looking into her eyes, I can see the confusion there. I'm sure my face is mirroring hers because I'm as confused as fuck. I've never felt this type of jealousy or possession for a woman. I sure as fuck haven't gotten hard just from watching one walk around waiting on tables.

Finally, I break the silence. "Honey, I don't know what this is, but there's something about you that brings out the possessive asshole in me. I'm not trying to manhandle you. You can trust me and my club. No one will hurt you there. I won't fire you, and if you want to wait tables, that's fine. Just expect me to be right next to you while you do it. I just know if I can get you behind the bar, there will be less of a chance of someone trying to cop a feel, or worse."

She rolls her eyes. "No one is going to try and touch me."

175

I don't know how she hasn't noticed it, but every man in the club would have her if they were given the chance. Frustrated, I growl, "Fine. You want to wait tables, do it. I'll murder the first bastard that puts his hands on you."

"Smoky," she huffs out, and I swear my whole body tenses from hearing my name on her lips.

I loop her purse on her shoulder. "It's your call."

She shakes her head. "Fine, I'll learn to make drinks. But I'm not sleeping with you."

I smirk. "Oh, we'll definitely be doing more than sleeping."

I thought that would get a laugh out of her, but it doesn't. "Yeah, Smoky, that's just it. You want to fuck. I'm not into one-night stands."

She whirls around but I stop her with a hand to her shoulder. I press my body up against the back of hers. My muscles tense and my heart races. I brush her hair to the side and whisper into her ear. "Me either. Not with you. I'm playing for keeps."

She freezes against me and I just stand there enjoying her heated, curvy body against mine. She must feel my hard cock pressed against her tight ass, because she presses against me, but when I moan, she freezes and pulls away, walking out the door.

She stops outside. "Where's your car?"

4

HARPER

I KNOW THIS ISN'T SMART. I SHOULDN'T GO anywhere with him, but I feel more alive right now than I have in a long time. For some reason, I feel safe with him. I know he wants more, but that doesn't mean he's going to get it. I'm not up for being his toy or another notch in his bedpost.

He follows me out of the club and stops next to a big motorcycle. Turning to face him, I see him eyeing the hairband on my wrist, so I take it, pulling my hair up off my shoulders and tying it in a knot on my head. He sits down and straightens the bike, then holds his hand out to me.

I back away from his reach. "No way. I'm not getting on that," I tell him, pointing at the monstrosity between his legs.

"It's safe. I won't let anything happen to you," he assures me with his hand still outstretched.

I hesitantly take a step toward him and then stop and tug on the bottom of my jean skirt. "There's no way I can ride that with this on."

"C'mon, we'll stop at your house so you can change if you want. Swing your leg over."

"No, no, it's fine. I'll just wear this." It's not that I'm ashamed of where I live, but it's pretty rundown and I don't want even more pity from this man. I walk over to him and avoid his hand as I climb onto the back of the bike, doing my best to not show him or anyone else my underwear.

Once I'm seated, he reaches behind and grips the outside of my thighs. "Scoot in, honey. And hold on tight."

I slide forward until my thighs are gripping him and I can feel the roughness of his jeans against my inner thighs and panty-clad pussy.

He then grabs my arms and wraps them around his torso. I can feel him take a big breath and he mutters, "Lean when I lean."

I grip on to him, worried and a little scared about being on a motorcycle for the first time. He fires up the loud engine and in a mere second we're taking off down the road.

I rest my head against his back with my eyes clenched closed. Once we've ridden for a few miles, he grabs my hand and holds it against his chest. I take a deep breath and lay my cheek against his shoulder. I can almost feel myself weakening for him. I could get used to this. Being with Smoky makes me feel things I've never felt before. But almost instantly, my thoughts stray to yesterday and Kristy on his lap. Even though I try to stop it, I can't. I try my best to distance myself from him on the bike, but with one hand he grips me tighter.

If nothing else, I need to guard my heart. I can't physically distance myself from him, but I do mentally. The rest of the ride is tense.

He pulls into a gravel lot and stops outside a large building that looks like a warehouse. There are bikes lined up and down the side of the building.

As soon as he comes to a stop, I hop off the bike and barely catch myself before falling over. He reaches over to steady me before kicking the stand and getting off.

"What was that?" he asks me.

I can tell by the look in his eyes; I know exactly what he's talking about. But I act like I don't. "What?"

"You froze up on me. What's that about?"

I just shrug my shoulders. I really don't want to piss him off.

He steps toward me. "Honey, I can't stay out here all night."

"Sorry. It's nothing, okay?" I turn to walk away.

He grabs on to my arm. "No, it's not okay. What's going on in that pretty head of yours?"

179

"I'm sorry. I freaked out a little bit, but it's none of my business, so forget about it," I tell him hastily.

He just shakes his head, but doesn't release his grip on me. "Tell me."

"I started thinking about Kristy grinding on you and it made me think about how many other women have been on the back of your bike." I pull away from him and undo the tie from my hair, then shake it loose, doing my best to pretend that he's not staring a hole in me right now.

He crowds me again and I keep walking backward until my back is pressed against the wall and he's fitted himself standing between my thighs.

He puts his hands on the wall on each side of my head and looks right into my eyes. "You. You are the only woman that's been on the back of my bike. And I've done some fucked-up shit in my day, stuff I'm not proud of, but it's different now."

I don't catch myself before I roll my eyes at him.

He grips my chin in his fingers and pulls me toward him. "You have no reason to trust me now, but I'm going to prove to you that I can be the man you want… the man you need."

I look up at him with shock in my face. "Smoky… I just met you yesterday. You can't make promises like that."

He shakes his head. "I can and I just did."

He bends down to touch his lips against mine, but before he reaches me, I put my hand on his chest and push him away from me. I know he can overpower me, but he doesn't even try. He steps back, seemingly unfazed that I pushed him away.

He grabs my hand and starts toward the entrance. I'm running hot and then cold with all of this and wish I was home in my bed to try to figure it all out.

With his hand on the door, he pauses. "Stay by my side until I get you to Keeper."

When he pushes open the door and ushers me in, well, I didn't know what I expected, but it wasn't this. There are tattooed bikers everywhere. Women are walking around in clothes that barely cover them. Even though I shouldn't, I grab onto Smoky's arm and hold on to him. He puts his arm around my shoulder and walks me to the bar. The man pouring a drink looks up at us and a smile fills his face.

"So this is her?" the bartender asks Smoky.

Confused, I look over at Smoky, but he looks as confused as I am.

The man wipes his hands off on a towel and then gestures toward me. "The prospect you sent to watch her last night told me all about her. He's right, she's beautiful."

My cheeks flush, until I realize exactly what he said. I turn to Smoky. "You had someone follow me last night?"

Smoky shrugs his shoulders like it's nothing. "Yeah. I had to make sure you got home safe."

I just shake my head at him before turning back to the bartender. I hold my hand out to him. "Hi. I'm Harper."

He holds his hand out to me, until I hear a low growl coming from Smoky and then the man pulls his hand back and instead gives me a little wave. *What in the world is that?* I think to myself.

As if I asked it out loud, the man says, "So Smoky's claimed you. You're off limits?" he looks over to Smoky and Smoky nods at him with a glare in his eyes.

"Okay, well, I'm Keeper. It's nice to meet you, Harper."

I just look between the two of them, surprised by what's going on here.

Smoky finally unfolds his arms. "Keep, I need you to teach Harper the basics of tending bar. Nothing fancy, just the basics."

Keeper walks over and lifts a part of the bar up. "Come on in, then," he tells me.

I walk behind the bar and Keeper goes through instructions on what I need to be doing. My eyes keep flitting over to Smoky. Instead of talking to his friends or to any number of the women sitting around, he is staring at me as I work.

Nervousness sets in, but I fight it. I remind

myself that I need this job and pay close attention to what Keeper is telling me.

An hour goes by and Smoky has finally quit staring at me. He's now talking to the club president, Sniper. I look around the room and can't contain my surprise. My father always told me to avoid this club and the men in it, but since I've been here, they have all been super nice. Plus, even though Smoky is probably a womanizer, he has been good to me.

I finish serving two beers to men at the end of the bar and then walk back to Keeper. "So, are you married, Keeper?"

I don't know how, but Smoky hears me over the noise in the room. "It doesn't matter if he's married or not, you're taken," he bellows, and all the men turn to look at us.

I just turn my back to him. He's not going to play me. I keep reminding myself what kind of man he is.

I look up at Keeper questioningly.

He just smirks. But I also see sadness in his eyes. "Nope, not married."

I turn my head to the side. "Girlfriend?"

He shakes his head. "No girlfriend either."

When I just keep staring at him, I can tell he gets uncomfortable. "There's a girl that I like, but, well, it's not possible for me and her. And I just haven't found someone since her."

So there it is. I knew there was a sadness to him. I look over at Smoky and his eyes are on me again. He looks at me with so much understanding and compassion I have to turn away.

Luckily the crowd picks up and I stay busy as I help Keeper work the bar.

5

SMOKY

AFTER SITTING AROUND AT THE BAR ALL NIGHT AND watching Harper work, I finally convince her that it's time to leave. It wouldn't take much for me to just take her back to my bedroom here at the clubhouse, but I remind myself that I'm trying to be a gentleman here. The guys loved her and when Avery, Sniper's ol' lady, showed up, well they hit it off fast. I couldn't wipe the smile off my face as I watched her laughing in the corner.

If someone had told me last week that I would be ready to settle down, I would have told them to fuck off. But here I am today, with Harper on the back of my bike, and I'm ready to fully commit to her, make her pregnant, and keep her by my side forever.

I drive faster just thinking about it, causing her

to hold on tighter. I pull into the driveway of her house and help her off the bike.

"Okay, well thank you. I'll see you at work tomorrow," she says and takes off, walking up the sidewalk.

I follow behind her quickly. "What's the rush?"

She stops at the door. "Look, Smoky, I appreciate everything you're trying to do here. I really do. But I'm not interested in well, whatever this is you want."

She doesn't look me in the eye as she says it, but I can sense that she's hurt.

"Why not?" I ask her. I want to wrap my arms around her and hold her close, but I don't. I can tell if I push her too hard now, she's going to run.

She looks like she might ignore me, but then she looks at me sadly. "You do know that when I met you yesterday, Kristy was about to come riding your leg. I'm just not interested in getting involved in any of that. I'm trying to save my house right now, no matter if it is falling down around me."

I look at her house and even in the dark, I can see the falling banister and holes in the porch. I look back at her. I don't know what to tell her, because she's right. I have played around, but that's in my past. That was before her. I cup her chin and lift it, bringing her eyes to mine. I lean in and kiss her forehead and then pull away. "Don't give up on me yet, Harper."

She looks like she might argue, but instead, she nods her head, walks into her house and before she shuts the door, I hear her whisper, "Good night, Smoky."

I walk off her porch and look up at the house. There's a tarp covering one side of her roof and the shutters are barely hanging on.

Harper

I'M WOKEN up at six the next morning by what sounds like a hammer. I jump out of bed and run to look outside, forgetting that I'm wearing a T-shirt and panties and nothing else. As soon as I walk out of the house, I realize my mistake. I'm surrounded by most, if not all of the Exiled Guardians. Most of them I met last night. They all seem to stop what they're doing and stare back at me.

"Get back to work," I hear from the crowd and the men immediately go back to what they were doing. I discover that Keeper was the one that hollered, because he bolts up the steps and blocks my body with his. "Get inside, Harper."

"But…" I start to argue.

He shakes his head and starts pushing me toward the door, but he isn't quick enough. A truck pulls into the yard and Smoky is out of it and up the porch in two seconds flat. "Hands off, Keep."

I look over at Smoky and see anger in his face. I step around Keeper and get between the two men. "What is going on?" I ask him.

He doesn't answer me. He just looks down at my body and his mouth drops. I hate to admit it but my body reacts and my nipples pebble under his stare.

"Smoky, she heard us out here and came to check it out. I was trying to get her back inside away from the men, that's all," Keeper says. There's no fear in his voice. He just says it matter-of-factly.

Smoky still doesn't take his eyes off me. He huskily says, "Thanks, Keep. I've got her now."

Keeper strides off the porch and instantly Smoky moves in closer to me. His voice is almost deadly sounding and sends chills down my body. "Get in the house, Harper."

"But…" I start and then notice the vein in his neck bulging. "Wait, are you mad at me? What did I do?"

He steps closer to me, shielding me from his biker friends. "Get. In. The. House."

I turn away and walk into the house with him right on my tail. As soon as he shuts the door, I whip around. "I don't know why you're mad at me. You and your friends are at my house. What are they even doing out there?"

He takes a deep breath and his nostrils flare. "Go put some clothes on."

I shake my head and put my hands on my hips. "You can't boss me around, Smoky."

His gaze sweeps down my body and lingers on my hips. I gasp when I look down at myself. I hadn't realized when I put my hands on my hips that I had pulled my shirt up and am showing him my belly and my private parts. My threadbare white underwear doesn't leave much to the imagination.

My hands slide down my body and I cover myself. My mouth gapes as I stare back at him, embarrassment flushing my face.

He rolls his shoulders. "Last chance, Harper. I plan to do right by you, but there's only so much a man can take. Now all of my brothers have seen you like this and I'm debating on going out there and plucking each of their eyeballs out. So I tell you for the last time, go get dressed or I'm taking you to your bedroom."

I stand there and stare at him, debating with myself on what to do. It shouldn't be a question. I should do what he says, but there's something so tempting about waiting to see what he'll do.

He smirks at me. Well, I think it's a smirk with a hint of anger still, but he takes a step toward me and I jump away, running for the safety of my bedroom. I grab my clothes and run into the bathroom to take a quick shower.

6

SMOKY

SHE'S PISSED. I SWEAR I CAN ALMOST SEE STEAM
coming out of her ears. When I told her we were
fixing her roof and porch, she about went ballistic.
When I saw the condition of the inside of her
house, I moved a team of men inside, one of them
being Keeper. He's one of the main guys I trust
here. I mean, I trust all the brothers, but I know
Keeper will keep an eye on Harper.

She argued with me, threatened to call the
police and then finally went and pouted to Keeper. I
kept my distance from her. I'm still hot from this
morning. When I pulled in and saw Keeper with his
hands on her, I about lost my shit. Even though I
know I can trust him, it still went all through me.
And then when I discovered that she was wearing
only panties and a T-shirt, well, I wanted to murder
someone.

I didn't know if I wanted to bend her over my knee and spank her little ass or take her to the bedroom and pound my seed into her until she begged for mercy.

As I watch her help Keeper, I can't get my mind off living with her here. I know she's not going to let me move in, at least not yet, but I want to be with her and I don't want to stay at the Exiled Guardians club or at my apartment above the strip club. I want a house with her, a family and until I can get something built, this is going to be it.

I know she doesn't want bossy. I can tell she doesn't like being told what to do. I'm trying to hold back. I know I have a lot to prove to her and until I do, well, I'm willing to take it slow.

"Keep," I holler.

He walks over to me and when I catch Harper staring at me, she turns her head away quickly. I would chuckle at her antics if I still wasn't feeling remnants of anger toward my men. They saw her almost naked. I've watched them the rest of the day and they haven't even looked her way. I'm sure they know by now I would kill someone if they messed with her.

"What's up, Smoky?"

"I'm going to the department and hardware store. Can you keep an eye on Harper?"

I ask him.

He shrugs his shoulders. "Yeah, but she's getting ready to go to work, she said."

Fuck. "Can you take her there? I will bring the stuff here and drop it off before I go in."

He nods his head, but I can tell he has something to say. "What is it, Keep?"

"She's pretty upset about all this." He gestures around the house. "She thinks you're doing this out of pity."

I look him dead in the eye. "I'm not."

He looks at me, measuring my response. I should be pissed, but honestly, I'm glad Harper has someone else on her side besides me. Looking around the room, l can see that the whole club has her back.

He nods his head, then slaps me on the back. "I'll get her to work."

Harper

WHEN I CAME out of my bedroom from getting ready for work, Smoky was gone. I knew it as soon as I walked out. I don't know what to think about all of this. He's pretty much avoided me since this morning. However, I've felt his stare all day long. I've felt a pull in my lower belly and a tingle in my whole body every time I look at him.

"I'm going to work, Keeper. I'll see you later," I tell him as I walk past.

I wave at a few of the guys and keep moving.

"Hold up!" Keeper stands up, wiping his hands down his jeans. "Smoky asked me to take you to work."

"What?" I roll my eyes. "No way. You've already been working on my house all day. I don't need you to walk me to work. Plus, if he was so worried about me getting there, he should be here to take me." My face flushes, and I want to kick myself for saying that out loud.

I stride out the door and get as far as the sidewalk before Keeper catches up with me. "Do you feel better?"

"Maybe. No. Ugh, where is he? I need to get this settled. I can't afford for you to do all this work on my house, and I don't want his pity either." I keep walking and Keeper, with his long legs, keeps up with me easily.

"He doesn't pity you. It's not my place to say how he feels about you, but I will tell you that this is new to him too. Give him a chance, Harper." I stop and he walks about ten feet ahead of me before he stops and turns around. I want to ask him what he means, but I don't. I'm sure there's some kind of bro code or something going on here and well, honestly, I don't know if I'm ready to hear it yet.

"Well, c'mon, you got me walking here and I

don't walk anywhere. Let's go." He claps his hands together and I walk up beside him.

"I'm sorry. We should have brought your bike. I wasn't thinking. Now you have to walk back," I apologize.

"I don't have a death wish. There's no way I would put you on the back of my bike. Brother or no brother, Smoky would shoot me for that one."

"For riding on your bike?" I ask him incredulously. Surely he's joking.

"Harper, to us, it means something to let a woman on the back of your bike. You don't just let anyone. I've never had a woman behind me, and I don't think Smoky has either," he says as he opens the door to the bar.

I walk in next to him and stop and point to myself. "Me. I rode on the back of his bike," I admit.

He just smiles and shakes his head. "That right there should tell you something."

I thank him for walking me and refuse his offer to stay until Smoky gets here. "Teddy's here. I'll be fine."

He looks over at Teddy and snarls his nose up. Obviously, there's something going on there. "Don't trust Teddy. He's here, but there's something about him I don't trust."

I nod my head at him, thank him again and then watch as he walks back out the door.

I walk to the bar and put my purse under the counter. "Hey, Teddy."

"Hey," he answers. "I'm going to need you waiting tables. I've had two servers call in and I can't pull any dancers, not on the weekend."

I almost argue with him, but I can tell that's what he's expecting. I think for a second I should call Smoky, but I don't have his number and decide to just do what he's asking me.

I nod at him, grab an apron and tie it around my waist.

It's definitely busier on the weekends, I'm finding out. And rowdier. There's a lot more people here and I'm tense the whole time I trek back and forth between the table and the bar. I know when Smoky gets here, he's going to be mad, but regardless, I have to make money.

7

SMOKY

IT TOOK ME LONGER THAN I THOUGHT IT TO PICK up everything and take it back to her house. The stuff that wouldn't fit in the truck I paid extra to have delivered tonight.

As soon as the boys unloaded my truck, I drove the five minutes to the club.

When I walk in I know something is wrong. I look at the bar and Teddy and Kristy are standing behind it. I look around the room and finally spot Harper.

As soon as I do, I start walking toward her, and as if she senses me, she turns around and looks straight at me.

I watch as an arm sneaks around her waist and pulls her down. Her eyes widen and I can see the fear from across the room. I make my way through the throng of people, watching helplessly as she struggles in the man's grasp. His other arm comes around her and grabs her breast as she winces in pain.

Mother fucker. I start pushing people left and right and before I reach her, the man holding her spots me and releases her. It doesn't stop me. I barrel into him, taking us both flying back onto the table. I pummel him with my fist and don't stop until three men drag me off. I stand up and turn to our bouncer, but before I jump on to him for not stopping this before it happened, I point to the man on the table. "Take him outside and make sure he never comes back. Take his friends with him."

I look at Harper, standing there and trembling like a leaf. "Aw, honey." I walk toward her but before I get to her, she runs toward me and into my open arms. I don't even hesitate. I lift her up into my arms and stride across the room. Everyone moves out of the way as we walk by and I take her up the back stairs to my apartment. When I get inside, I take her straight to the bedroom and set her down on her unsteady feet.

I pull her T-shirt up, but she puts her hand out to stop me.

"Honey, it's okay," I assure her. "I just want to make sure you're all right."

She releases her hold on me and lets me take her shirt off. I unfasten her bra and gasp at the bruising that is already forming on her large, round breast. "I should have killed the fucker," I grunt.

I stroke my finger across her bruised skin softly. She arches against me, but I pull gently away. She pulls out of reach then. "I'm fine, Smoky."

I should tell her that she was supposed to be behind the bar, but I don't want her to feel like I'm blaming her for this. No, that will be a conversation for another day.

She turns her back to me and I see the wince on her face as she turns. I stroke my hand down her side and see a faint bruise on her ribs.

I step toward her, putting my body against hers. I circle my arms around her because I have to, because I need her right now... even if she thinks she doesn't need me.

"Baby, please let me take care of you. Please. It kills me that he was hurting you and I couldn't get to you in time. I won't do anything else, just care for you. I promise."

She turns in my arms and I try to ignore the feeling of her bare breasts pressed against my chest. "It's not your fault, Smoky. I knew I should have been behind the bar, but Teddy said he needed me on the floor."

I take a deep breath and slowly release it. It looks like I'll be looking for a new assistant because he did the exact opposite of what I told him to do.

I lay my head against hers. She has the smell of beer and sweat from the man that grabbed her.

I take her hand and walk her to the bathroom. I turn the water on and then help her undress.

I know she's uncomfortable with this by the way she tries to shield her body from me. I grab her hands and stop her. "No, honey. It's not about that. I want you. There's no doubt I want you, but right now, I only want to help you."

She nods her head and drops her arms to her sides.

I help her into the shower stall and quickly remove my clothes while her back is turned. I climb in behind her and she stands there with her head back and the water beating down on her. The glistening water rolls down her body and my cock hardens at the sight of her curves. My imagination didn't do her justice. She's breathtaking.

My hands go to her shoulders and I caress them until she's no longer tight. Then I take a sponge hanging on the wall and coat it with soap. I run it down her back, across her rounded ass, and down her legs. She turns to face me and my cock twitches. She gasps when she sees me naked, but at least she doesn't run from the bathroom. I stroke her breasts, her belly, between her thighs and down her legs. She's arching toward me and I know that if I was a lesser man, I would take her right now, standing up against the shower wall.

When I stand back up, I put shampoo in my hand and turn her around to wash and condition her hair. She moans as I massage her scalp. Once I rinse her off, she turns to me and grabs the sponge off the wall.

I smile at her, secretly happy that we're making progress.

I take the sponge from her. "Baby, if you touch me right now, I won't be able to stop myself."

I WASH QUICKLY, tugging on my cock a few times as I clean myself. She watches me, her eyes big and hungry.

I throw it down and turn off the water. I dry her quickly and can barely take my eyes off her bruises.

I pull a T-shirt out of the drawer and slide it over her towel-covered head. I pull on a pair of boxers and then lead her over to the bed, pulling down the covers and helping her sit down.

"Have you eaten?" I towel dry her hair and then unwrap it, handing her my brush.

She takes it and starts brushing out her hair. "I ate lunch earlier today."

"I'll be right back."

I go into the kitchen and quickly make her something to eat.

When I walk back into the bedroom, she's

looking up at me with hooded eyes. "Here, honey. Sit up."

She scoots backwards and leans against the headboard. When I put the plate on her lap, she grins. "A grilled cheese sandwich?"

I smile at seeing the happy expression on her face. "I take it you like them?"

She takes a bite and moans around the gooey cheese. "It's my favorite."

I sit at the end of the bed and watch her devour her sandwich. She's not embarrassed by me watching her, and I love that about her.

"Is that for me too?" she asks, pointing at my hands.

I smirk, not even realizing that I had a glass of milk in my hands the whole time.

I hand it to her and she takes a big gulp before putting it on the table beside the bed. I get up and reach for it.

She curls to her side. "Where are you going?"

I stroke the hair away from her face and look at her lovingly. "I'm going to let you rest."

"Stay with me. Will you, Smoky? Please?"

I know if I lie down with her, I will feel temptation like no other, but I can't tell her no.

I set the glass down and walk around the bed to lie on top of the cover.

She turns over to face me. "You'll get cold."

HOPE FORD

"I doubt that," I tell her because right now I'm burning up.

She stares at me and I can tell her mind is working a mile a minute.

"Ask me," I tell her.

She smiles at me. "Okay. Why are you helping me with the house?"

I shrug my shoulders. "Because I want to."

She slides an inch toward me. "It's going to take me a while to pay you back. You know that, right?"

I smile as she scoots a little closer to me. I don't know if she realizes she's doing it or not.

"Why would you pay me back? I'll be living there too. At least until we get the house built," I tell her honestly.

"House? What house?" she exclaims.

"The one we're going to live in," I tell her.

She starts to ask another question but I lean over and kiss her softly on the lips. Reluctantly, I realize too late that touching her was a bad decision. I want her and this isn't helping. I pull back. "Go to sleep, honey. We'll talk about everything in the morning."

She nods her head and barely covers her mouth before she's yawning. I pull the covers more securely around her and watch as she drifts off. When she grins in her sleep, I know I'm making the right decision by her. I may have just met her, but I can't imagine my life without her in it.

8

HARPER

I RAISE MY HEAD OFF OF SOMETHING THAT FEELS like a furnace. When I see that I'm sprawled on top of Smoky, my first instinct is to slide off and to the other side of the bed. But something stops me. Maybe it's his hand that is snug against my back, holding and protecting me. Or maybe it's the feelings I have for him. But whatever it is, I lay my head down and bask in the joy of being in his arms. I move my leg a little and he moans underneath me. I raise my head and look at him, but he's still sleeping.

Slowly, I raise myself off of him and slide down the bed. His cock is hard and poking out the elastic band of his shorts. I eye his manhood and lick my lips when a drop of precum glistens on the tip. I lean up, not about to stop myself from getting a taste of him. As soon as his flavor hits my tongue, I open my mouth wider and pull him into my mouth.

He startles then, his body jerking and unintentionally pushing farther into my mouth. I look up at his face and he's wide awake, his brown eyes almost black with lust.

"Harper," he groans.

I lean up then, getting on my knees. I smile at him before taking him again, this time pulling him to the back of my throat. When I swallow him, he throws his head back and groans. I back off before deep throating him again. When I gag on his huge cock, which is expanding even more in my mouth, he grunts and pulls me off his rod and up his body. My legs are nudged apart and I'm straddling him, with his cock pressed against my butt cheeks.

"Harper, I want you. I want this. Fuck, I want it more than anything I've ever wanted in my life. But I need you to be sure, because once I'm between your thighs, there's no turning back. You're mine."

He looks so serious that I can't help but laugh.

He grabs my hips in a tight grip.

I just smile at him before I whip my shirt off over my head. Looking down at him, I tell him. "It's too late. You're already between my legs."

I lean down and kiss his lips. His tongue plunges into my mouth and meets mine. I push my bare pussy against him, rocking back and forth.

Cupping my ass, he flips his body over until he's

lying on top of me. "Harper, I need you now." He kisses my mouth, my cheek, my collarbone, and my breast.

"Take me, Smoky. I need you too."

His hand goes down between us and plunges into my drenched heat. Like a damn hussy, I gyrate my hips against his palm. Already, I'm close to the brink and desire shoots through me as I come on his hand while he plunges his fingers into me. My hands tighten around him and my fingernails claw into his back. He trembles then, the pain and ecstasy too much.

He spreads me open and fits himself against my soaked opening. I take him in, feeling him stretching me to his girth. He moves slowly but the pressure is too much and I tighten around him as I feel the pulsating vibrations of his loaded cock as he seats himself inside me. When he's buried to the hilt, his head falls down on mine. He takes a deep breath, trying to control himself.

I raise my legs up and bring them around him, opening myself even more to him. He pulls out, the slick sounds of him sliding deeply back into me filling the room.

He pounds into me, our bodies slapping against each other. His cock twitches inside of me and my pussy squeezes him as another orgasm takes hold. When I arch my body, I bear down on him with a vise grip as he moves in and out of me. I grunt and groan but I don't stop. My whole body tautens as his throbbing dick pushes in and out of me.

He comes then, grunting his climax into my mouth as he buries himself to the hilt inside me.

He stays there and I wrap my arms and legs around him, not wanting him to move. This, right here, is perfection.

He groans then, and with one more twitch of his dick, he slowly pulls out of me.

Lying down beside me, he pulls me into his arms and kisses me.

His phone dings on the table and he lifts up and looks at it. He smiles widely at me. "Get dressed, honey. Our home is ready."

I raise my head to look at him and admire his fine ass as he tugs on a pair of jeans. I roll over on the bed. "Normally, I would be curious about what you're talking about. But right now, I don't think I could move if I wanted to."

He sits on the edge of the bed and gives my ass a smack. "C'mon, I have a surprise for you."

Smoky

IT TOOK SOME WORK, but I finally got her out of bed. I help her into my truck and we drive the few blocks to her house.

When we pull in, her mouth gapes.

"What in the world?"

The house looks completely different. It took them almost twenty-four hours, but there is a vast improvement in the house just from yesterday.

The siding has been washed, the shutters redone, the porch fixed. Hell, someone even planted flowers along the walkway.

"Smoky, oh my God, what did you do?"

"Honey, I was with you. This was all my brothers. They did this… for us." I tell her that because I have no doubt now that I will be moving in here with her.

We walk up the front steps and she takes her time looking at everything. She wipes away a tear rolling down her cheek. I just smile at her, grab her hand and pull her to the door. I unlock it and stand back to let her in.

Even I'm surprised at the inside. They did an amazing job on such short notice. I look into the kitchen and notice they even installed all the new appliances and the new couch was delivered. There are more flowers, and it makes me think that I probably need to thank Avery. This looks like it had her touch on it.

Harper walks room to room, speechless. She opens the guest bedroom, looks in and slams it shut quickly before turning back to me.

"Oh yeah, I should have warned you about that." I laugh.

"Is that a baby crib in there?" she asks me with shock on her face.

I grab her around the waist. "Honey, we're getting married, and we're going to have a family. I saw that yesterday and I had to have it. If you don't like it, we can take it back and you can pick out what you want."

She opens the door again and we peek in at the dark stained crib. She looks up at me and puts her hands on each side of my jaw. "It's perfect, Smoky."

EPILOGUE

SMOKY

Three Months Later

IT'S ALL COME FULL CIRCLE. I MARRIED HARPER three weeks from the day I met her. I moved in with her and even though I offered to build her a house, she didn't want me to. She loves the house we're in and isn't ready to leave it. Which is fine by me. I don't care where we live as long as I'm with her.

She's made good friends with all of the ol' ladies. We're at the Exiled Guardians club celebrating Sniper's half-sister Lilly's return.

All the women are sitting in the corner talking. Some of the sweet butts are here but I don't pay them any mind. Not anymore. Not when I have my whole world right in front of me.

I lean down and kiss her shoulder. "Do you want something from the bar?"

She smiles at me. "I'll get it. I want to talk to Keeper anyway."

I simply nod my head at her. She and Keeper have become good friends, and I'm okay with it. I watch her walk away and can't help but admire the way her ass fills out her jeans. She told me she's got something to tell me later, but I already know what it is. She's pregnant. She hasn't had a period since the first month we were together. And now, well, I can tell her body is changing. But I don't want to ruin her surprise. I'll wait until she's ready. I hope she knows me well enough by now that when she tells me, she better be ready, because nothing will stop me from claiming her sweet pussy right then.

She sits down at the bar, and I turn to Sniper and Lilly.

***

Harper

"HEY, KEEP, WHAT'S UP?"

He smiles at me, but it doesn't quite reach his eyes.

"Are you okay?" I ask him.

He shrugs his shoulders and pours a beer, sliding it over to me. I almost lift it to my mouth and stop. "You know what? I'll take a water."

He looks at me knowingly and I fight the blush on my cheeks. He sets a water down in front of me.

I take a swig and look up at Keeper.

He's looking behind me and the look on his face is filled with longing and dare I say it, love.

I look over my shoulder and right then Lilly lifts her eyes to Keeper and a pretty blush crosses her cheeks. I gasp and whip back around.

"It's her. She's the one that got away," I say to him excitedly.

He silences me with a painful look. "Don't, Harper. It's not like that. Just let it be."

"But, Keeper, I don't understand," I insist.

"Let it go," he says in a husky voice.

I have so many questions, but I don't ask him. I can see he's hurting and I don't want to make it worse. I nod my head at him. "Okay. I'm here if you want to talk."

He smirks. "I'm a badass biker, Harper. I don't talk about my feelings."

I just shake my head at him because he may be a badass, but he's a "good" badass.

I jump as arms go around my neck. Smoky kisses my neck. "You ready to go home, honey?"

I nod my head, because truly I am excited to go home and tell him that he's going to be a daddy.

I'm not even worried about it. He's made it known since the day after I met him that he wants us to have a baby.

I swing the chair around and loop my arms around his neck, then kiss his lips. "I'm ready, baby."

The End

The Exiled Guardians Series is complete. Go to https://authorhopeford.com/books/ for more information.

FREE BOOKS

Want FREE BOOKS?
Go to www.authorhopeford.com/freebies

JOIN ME!

JOIN MY NEWSLETTER & READERS GROUP

www.AuthorHopeFord.com/Subscribe

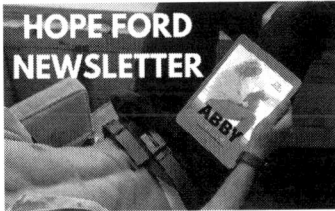

JOIN MY READERS GROUP ON FACEBOOK

www.FB.com/groups/hopeford

Find Hope Ford at www.authorhopeford.com

ABOUT THE AUTHOR

USA Today Bestselling Author Hope Ford writes short, steamy, sweet romances. She loves tattooed, alpha men, instant love stories, and ALWAYS happily ever afters. She has over 100 books and they are all available on Amazon.

To find me on Pinterest, Instagram, Facebook, Goodreads, and more:

www.AuthorHopeFord.com/follow-me

Printed in Great Britain
by Amazon